For more than forty years,
Yearling has been the leading name
in classic and award-winning literature
for young readers.

Yearling books feature children's
favorite authors and characters,
providing dynamic stories of adventure,
humor, history, mystery, and fantasy.

Trust Yearling paperbacks to entertain,
inspire, and promote the love of reading
in all children.

The Five Ancestors

THE FIVE ANCESTORS

蛇 Snake

Jeff Stone

A YEARLING BOOK

for my brothers,
Joe and Jaysen

Published by Yearling, an imprint of Random House Children's Books
a division of Random House, Inc., New York

Visit us on the Web! www.randomhouse.com/kids and www.fiveancestors.com

Educators and librarians, for a variety of teaching tools, visit us at
www.randomhouse.com/teachers

ISBN: 978-0-375-83076-1

Reprinted by arrangement with Random House Books for Young Readers

Printed in the United States of America

February 2007

10 9

First Yearling Edition

A Legendary pursuit!

With their enemy hot on their heels, three of Cangzhen's young warrior monks flee to the famed Shaolin Temple for sanctuary. Upon their arrival, they discover to their horror that Shaolin has been destroyed! Then the young monks hear rumors of a bandit gang whose leader was a frequent visitor to Cangzhen. Perhaps he holds the key to their destiny as . . .

the Five Ancestors.

Henan Province, China
4344–Year of the Dog
(1646 AD)

PROLOGUE

Eight-year-old Seh slid his lanky body along the enormous rafter high above the Cangzhen banquet table, doing his best to disturb as little dust as possible. Even in a room as dark as this, Grandmaster would notice a single particle drifting toward the floor. Grandmaster was that good.

But Seh was better. As long as he didn't lose focus.

Once in position, Seh stretched to his full length and flattened himself against the top of the wooden beam. He began to slow his breathing. His heart rate slowed to that of a hibernating reptile beneath a sheet of ice. Seh began to wait.

An hour later, Grandmaster entered the room. Although Grandmaster didn't say a word, Seh knew exactly who it was. He sensed powerful chi—life energy—

radiating from Grandmaster's body like heat from the sun.

Seh slowed his breathing further. He needed to keep his heart rate as slow as possible so that the chi coursing through his own nervous system would not alert Grandmaster to his presence. As long as he remained calm, Grandmaster would not detect him. Dragon-style kung fu masters like Grandmaster and Seh's brother Long possessed tremendous amounts of chi, but they weren't particularly good at detecting it in others. Snake stylists like Seh, however, were masters at detecting the most minute amounts in any living creature.

As Grandmaster stepped farther into the hall, Seh heard a second man stop in the doorway. Seh took a long, slow breath.

Seh focused on the visitor and noticed something strange. The man seemed to possess no chi at all, which was impossible. All living things possessed chi. This could mean only one thing—Grandmaster's visitor was masking his, something only snake-style kung fu masters knew how to do. And the only snake-style master to ever visit Grandmaster in the middle of the night was—

One corner of Seh's mouth slid down his long face in a lopsided frown. He peeked over the rafter toward the moonlit doorway and his eyes confirmed what the pit of his stomach already knew. Grandmaster's visitor was a man named Mong, a local bandit leader. Mong meant "python" in Cantonese. Seh had had more than one humiliating encounter with the gigantic snake-style kung fu master over the years, and he had no interest in seeing the man again.

Grandmaster turned to Mong and whispered, "Do you sense that we are alone?"

Seh remained perfectly still and watched Mong scan the room. Seh was enshrouded in darkness and positioned at a severe angle from the doorway. He was certain he was invisible. Yet when Mong's eyes hesitated as they passed over the rafter, Seh knew he had been discovered. Mong had sensed his chi. Seh was about to begin his retreat when Mong turned toward Grandmaster.

"Yes, we are alone," Mong said. "Nothing here but the occasional small pest." Mong entered the hall and closed the doors behind him.

Seh clenched his teeth. Pest? he thought. Seh wondered whether Mong was trying to make him angry so that his heart rate would rise and he'd reveal himself. There was nothing Seh hated more than getting caught when he was sneaking around.

Seh did his best to stay calm. He needed to stay focused. He suspected that Grandmaster and Mong were both dealers of secrets. They would trade them like other people traded gold for silk or silver for swords. Seh wanted those secrets. Especially if they involved him and his brothers—and Seh had a hunch they would.

"What news do you bring?" Grandmaster asked Mong. "And what might you require in return for sharing it?"

"I have no new information," Mong replied. "This visit is purely personal."

Grandmaster nodded. "The boys are progressing well," he said. "I suspect they'll all be masters in record time. Though I worry about the maturity level of some of them. Fu and Malao in particular come to mind."

Mong chuckled. "I imagine Fu and Malao could be a handful, especially if they're together. How is Long doing?"

"Very well," Grandmaster replied. "He is wise beyond his years."

"That's good," Mong said. "And what about the girl?"

"Hok is progressing well, too."

Seh nearly tumbled off the rafter. Hok? A girl? He took a long, slow breath. Mong was trying to break his concentration, and that last bit of information had nearly done it. But Seh was certain he could remain calm, no matter what Mong said next.

He was wrong.

"And what about my son?" Mong asked.

No . . . , Seh thought. It can't be. . . . He swallowed hard as his heart began to beat in his throat. He couldn't control it. He glared down at Mong, wondering if it was a trick.

It wasn't.

Grandmaster glanced up at the beam. "Seh is also progressing well. Perhaps too well. I worry about him most of all."

HENAN PROVINCE, CHINA
4348—YEAR OF THE TIGER
(1650 AD)

After years of sneaking around, few things surprised twelve-year-old Seh anymore. The attack on Cangzhen, however, had caught him completely off guard.

As Seh slipped through the undergrowth, leaving the destruction far behind, he knew exactly what he needed to do—get more information. Spying on Grandmaster had taught him that the more information a person had, the more influence that person had. And with enough influence, a single person could convince many others to join his cause.

Seh knew he was going to need help. A lot of help.

Ying was going to pay for this.

Four hours from Cangzhen's burning courtyards, Seh stopped at the edge of a moonlit clearing. The treeless expanse had been formed by a gigantic rock slide, originating somewhere higher up the face of ShiShan Mountain, looming to his right. Mount ShiShan had long been rumored to be the home of numerous organizations that preferred to operate outside the normal boundaries of society and law. Its shadow had been the perfect location for a temple like Cangzhen.

Seh had overheard Grandmaster mention several times that this clearing was a secret meeting place. Seh wondered if he met anyone here, which side of the shadows they would reside on. He tightened the sash around his orange robe and stepped out into the open. The pit of his stomach immediately began to tingle. He sensed *chi*. Human *chi*. Someone was out there.

Seh spun around and slipped beneath a large slab of stone jutting out from a pile of boulders. He lay on his side, curled into a ball. It wasn't a perfect hiding place, but it would have to do.

Seh rested his cheek on the cold, rocky ground and held his breath. He did not feel any vibrations. No one was moving. At least not yet.

He raised his head slightly and began to breathe . . . slowly . . . deeply. He scanned the moonlit surroundings, and his ears strained to pick up any sounds. Nothing. There was still a fair amount of *chi* in the air, but Seh could not pinpoint the source.

And then something stirred in the tree line across the clearing. Seh locked on its position. He hissed softly and compressed every muscle in his body, poised to strike.

"I hope you took your shoes off before crawling into my living room," a nasal voice said from across the clearing. "I'd hate for you to dirty up the place."

Beneath the slab of stone, Seh blinked twice. He had a hard time believing what he was hearing—or seeing.

A strange-looking man stepped from the tree line into the moonlight and began to wobble directly toward Seh's hiding place. The man was of average height, but he had curiously short arms and legs. His stubby legs worked double time to move him along at a normal pace, and his long torso swayed as he walked. Though the air was chilly, the man wore only a tattered vest and threadbare silk pants torn off at the knees. He was streaked with dirt from head to toe, and his long, thinning hair was matted with bits of leaves and twigs. A similarly long, thin mustache hung down on either side of his tiny mouth, stretching almost to his chest.

As the man scurried forward, he scratched his extremely wide nose with a dirty fingernail. His nose looked like it had been pounded flat with a hammer.

Seh grimaced. He had never seen a man so ugly or so filthy. The man didn't smell so great, either.

The dirty man stopped in front of the stone slab. He peered into the moon shadows beneath and frowned. "That was a joke, kid. Don't you find it funny?"

Seh didn't reply. He stared hard at the disgusting man.

"My, you're a serious one," the man said. "Come

on out, then. Let's forget the small talk and get down to business. I suppose you have information to exchange."

Seh didn't reply.

"People only come here for one reason," the man said. "Especially in the middle of the night. Do you have information to exchange or not?"

"I might," Seh replied.

"You might," the man repeated, shaking his head. He knelt down and leaned toward Seh. "Get out of there."

Seh compressed his body and sank farther under the slab. He wedged his back between the heavy rock and the ground.

"If you want information, we're going to do things my way," the man said. "We're going to play a little game. You'll stand a much better chance if you crawl out of there. Trust me."

"Trust you?" Seh said. "I don't even know you."

The dirty man sighed and one of his hands shot forward, grabbing Seh's wrist with an iron grip. Seh expanded his body and locked himself into place, but the man was unbelievably strong. Rock and stony earth scratched Seh as he was dragged out from under the slab. He writhed and twisted and tried to pull free, but the dirty man held fast.

Seh grunted as he struggled to his feet. "Don't . . . make me . . . hurt you."

The dirty man laughed. "Hurt me? I'm counting on it! *One new thing you'll know for every solid blow!* That's the name of the game. Understand?"

"No . . . ," Seh replied, struggling to pull his arm free. "I strongly suggest you release me. This is your last warning—"

"That's the spirit!" the man said. "Fight back, and perhaps I'll answer some of your questions. *One new thing you'll know for every solid blow!* If you land a solid blow, I have to answer one question. Likewise, if I land a solid blow, you have to answer one of my questions. I've been playing this game with travelers for years, which is probably why my nose looks the way it does. Some people think I've been hit in the head a few too many times, and perhaps they're right. But for some reason, I can't seem to stop playing. I love it! I find friendly sparring matches a great way to exchange information with strangers. Why, just the other day, I—*umpfff!*"

The man's words were cut short by a lightning-quick front kick to the lips.

Seh returned his foot to the ground and the pressure on his arm released. He jerked his wrist free and took a step back.

The dirty man rubbed his jaw and looked down at Seh's foot. "Very nice kick!" he said with a bloody grin. *"One new thing you'll know for every solid blow!* For that lovely bit of footwork, I'll answer one question. Go ahead, ask me anything."

Seh stared at the man's happy, bleeding face. "Who *are* you?"

"My name is NgGung." The dirty man bowed.

"Your name is . . . Centipede?" Seh said. "That's Cantonese."

"That's right," NgGung said. "I have a Cantonese animal name, just like you, *Seh*."

Seh's eyes widened. "How do you know my name?"

NgGung laughed. "Not yet, kid. *One new thing you'll know for every solid blow!*"

"But—"

NgGung lunged forward and slammed the heel of his palm into the center of Seh's chest. Seh stumbled backward, certain he'd never been hit that hard before. NgGung's hand was as hard as stone.

NgGung laughed again. "Yes! A solid blow for me! My turn to ask a question. Let's see. . . . Since you're here, I can only assume something has happened at Cangzhen. Ummm . . . Did someone attack the temple?"

Seh coughed and rubbed his aching chest. "What? Yes. My former brother Ying, he—"

NgGung raised a filthy hand. "Rules are rules. You just answered my question. More than one, actually. I'm not entitled to any more information. That is, until I hit you again!" NgGung lunged at Seh.

Seh reacted without thinking. As NgGung came at him, Seh spun to one side and dropped low to the ground. He extended all four fingers on one hand and pulled them tightly together, bending his wrist ninety degrees. He tucked his thumb against the side of his hand, cocked the snake-head fist back to his ear, and thrust it forward with all his might straight into NgGung's midsection.

Seh's hand bounced off NgGung's stomach like a spear tip bouncing off a thick plate of iron. Seh felt the reverberation all the way up to his elbow. He scowled and looked at NgGung, who stopped his attack and took a step back. NgGung grinned and opened his vest.

Seh stared in disbelief. Even in the moonlight, he could tell that NgGung's stomach was unlike any he had ever seen. NgGung's abdominal muscles were thick like iron bands and perfectly formed. They looked like the segmented armor of an insect.

NgGung pointed to a red mark just below his belly button. "Look here!" he said excitedly. "Your strike landed right on top of my *dan tien*—my *chi* center. You have excellent aim, my friend. That blow would have brought most men to their knees. However, I'd venture to say that that one hurt you more than it hurt me! Even so, we'll count it as a solid blow because of your amazing accuracy. In response to your question, I learned your name from Mong."

"Mong?" Seh said. "How do—"

NgGung smiled and shook his head. *"One new thing you'll know for every solid blow!"* He took a step toward Seh, cocking one leg and one arm back.

Seh hissed. It was time to bring this game to an end.

NgGung whipped his body around with amazing speed, extending one arm and one leg. Seh jumped over NgGung's spinning kick and barely raised his forearms in time to block NgGung's spinning arm.

The impact of NgGung's arm against Seh's forearms sent Seh tumbling sideways through the air. Seh hit the ground on one shoulder and tucked into a roll. He popped up onto his feet and turned to face NgGung.

NgGung was grinning from ear to ear. Seh was not. His forearms were killing him. NgGung's arm, like his stomach, was as hard as iron. Seh realized NgGung must practice Iron Shirt kung fu. Hitting any part of NgGung's upper body would be useless.

"Well done!" NgGung said, walking toward Seh. "That was definitely a block on your part. No new information for me from that exchange! Get your hands up. Here I come again!"

NgGung began to spin.

Seh knew he couldn't go blow for blow with NgGung. He would end up breaking his hands—or worse. As NgGung neared, Seh got an idea. He leaned forward as though he were about to counterattack, but the moment NgGung's spinning arm and leg were about to connect with him, Seh launched himself up and backward. Seh easily cleared NgGung's leg, but NgGung's fist glanced off the side of Seh's slick bald head—just as Seh had hoped. Seh slumped to the ground and lay perfectly still.

NgGung stopped spinning and looked down at Seh. "Well, well," he said, stepping up to Seh in the moonlight. "This is a bit of a surprise. I thought you would have given me a better run."

NgGung kicked Seh hard in the stomach. It took every bit of willpower Seh had to leave his muscles loose and not tighten them against the kick. Seh wanted NgGung to be convinced he was unconscious.

It worked. NgGung sighed and straddled Seh to pick him up. As soon as Seh sensed NgGung bending over him, Seh struck.

Seh snapped his eyes open and jammed the first two fingers of both hands into pressure points on NgGung's inner thighs.

NgGung's legs buckled. As NgGung sank toward the ground, Seh rolled onto his back and pulled his knees into his chest. Then he slid his legs along either side of NgGung's body and locked his ankles around NgGung, scissor-style.

Squeezing as hard as he could, Seh twisted sideways, pinning NgGung's arms to his sides and his back to the ground. At the same time, Seh leaned toward NgGung's head. Seh formed a hook with the first two fingers on one hand and slammed his snake-fang fist against the jugular vein on NgGung's neck.

"I've had enough of your game," Seh hissed. "Answer my questions and I'll consider letting you live to play another day."

NgGung laughed as he struggled to breathe. "My, my, my . . . such a serious . . . young man! No matter . . . you've tricked me . . . fair and square. I should have . . . expected as much . . . from a serpent. On my honor . . . release me . . . and I'll tell you . . . anything you want to know."

"Anything?" Seh asked.

"Yes . . ."—NgGung chuckled as he gasped for air—". . . anything."

Seh unhooked his ankles and kicked NgGung

away. NgGung pushed himself into a sitting position and smiled. Even in the moon shadows, Seh could see that NgGung was missing several teeth.

"Whew!" NgGung said, taking a deep breath. "Now tell me that wasn't fun!"

"Hardly," Seh said, sitting up. "I nearly broke my hand on your stomach."

NgGung laughed. "That Iron Shirt training sure comes in handy. So, what is it you would like to know?"

Seh paused a moment. He thought about why he had come to the clearing. He needed information, and he needed help. NgGung had mentioned Mong. Though Seh wasn't crazy about the idea, he realized Mong might be a good person to start with.

"Tell me about Mong," Seh said. "How do you know him?"

"He's one of my closest friends," NgGung said. "We grew up together at Cangzhen Temple."

"Cangzhen?" Seh asked. "Mong was a warrior monk?"

"Of course," NgGung replied. "Where do you think he got his Cantonese animal name?"

Seh blinked. He had never thought about that possibility before. It made sense, especially considering Mong's skills.

"So, you were a warrior monk, too?" Seh asked.

NgGung made a fist with his right hand and pressed his knuckles into the palm of his open left hand. He raised his fingertips toward the sky and placed his "folded" hands in front of his heart. This unique hand fold was the manner in which Cangzhen monks greeted one another. NgGung nodded.

Seh nodded back. "I've never heard of centipede-style kung fu," Seh said.

"We are a rare breed," NgGung replied with a chuckle. He unfolded his hands.

"How did you detect me earlier?" Seh asked.

"Centipede stylists don't possess an extraordinary amount of *chi,* but we can sense those who do. As you probably know, snakes and dragons have far more *chi* than anyone else. That's how I detected you hiding under the slab, and that's also how I knew you were a snake. No offense, but a dragon would never have hidden. A dragon would have stood his ground and faced me head-on."

Seh frowned.

"Speaking of dragons," NgGung said, "you said that Ying attacked Cangzhen. I can't believe he was that foolish. How badly did you beat him?"

"Beat him?" Seh said.

"Yes," NgGung replied. "The group he led through here yesterday looked pathetic."

"You *saw* him coming?" Seh said, standing up. "Why didn't you warn us?"

NgGung's dirty eyebrows rose. "I did. Ying's party didn't look too threatening, but I told your Grandmaster nonetheless. What happened?"

"What happened?" Seh said. "Ying destroyed Cangzhen!"

NgGung's eyes widened. "How? Ying only had a hundred or so men with him."

Seh's jaw tightened. "Ying had far more men than that, and many of them carried *qiang*s."

"*Qiang*s?" NgGung said. "*That's* what must have been in that big cart his men were pulling. It was too well guarded for me to sneak a peek. I'm really sorry, Seh. How many of you survived?"

Seh lowered his eyes. "I think only five of us escaped. There's a chance Grandmaster is still alive, but I doubt it. He looked exhausted when I last saw him, and he was about to fight Ying. Ying looked ready for him."

"Ying has been preparing to fight Grandmaster ever since he left the temple a year ago," NgGung said. "He's still young, but he may be the best fighter to ever come out of Cangzhen. I must find out what happened. You'll have to find Mong and tell him what's going on. Someone will have to warn the monks at Shaolin Temple, too. There might be something bigger going on."

"Shaolin?" Seh said.

"Yes," NgGung said, rubbing his thighs. "I'm sorry, but I don't have time to explain further. Find Mong, and he'll get you up to speed if he thinks you need to know the details."

"But—"

"We can't waste another moment, Seh. There's too much at stake. Believe me. Fortunately, Mong recently completed a mission nearby and he's on his way back to our stronghold. If you hurry, you can catch him. The stronghold is less than a day's travel from here. You'll have a much better chance of seeing him on the road than getting into the stronghold."

NgGung groaned and stood on shaky legs. "Ohhh, that double snake fist sure was a great move. I'll have to remember that." He grinned and began to wobble toward the tree line. "Wait here a moment."

NgGung returned with a grimy sack and tossed it to Seh. "For you."

Seh opened the sack and removed a blue robe made of fine silk. He also found matching blue pants and a blue silk hat, plus a pair of black cotton shoes.

"It's time to shed your orange robe," NgGung said. "Put it in the sack and hide it under the stone slab. I will dispose of it. Ying will have people looking every-where for you. While you wear those fancy clothes, do your best to act like an aristocrat. From what I've heard, it shouldn't be too difficult."

"What is *that* supposed to mean?" Seh asked.

"Nothing," NgGung said. "Forget it."

Seh ran his fingers over the fine cloth. "Are you sure you want me to take these? They must be worth a lot."

"They are," NgGung said. "But gold and silver mean nothing to me. I only kept those in case I needed to pretend to be something I am not. To tell you the truth, I'm glad you're taking them off my hands." NgGung pointed into the trees. "Go west about half a *li* and you'll find a wide trail that runs north to south.

Follow it north along the base of the mountain. I suggest you hurry. Mong and the boys are usually asleep at this hour, but they'll break camp soon after sunrise."

"I'll hurry," Seh said, still fingering the fine cloth. "Thank you."

NgGung bowed. "Safe travels, my friend. Tell Mong everything you told me and let him know that I saw—" NgGung paused and stared at Seh a moment, then shook his head. "Tell Mong that I saw Tonglong traveling with Ying."

"Praying Mantis?" Seh said.

"Yes, Praying Mantis."

"Who is he?"

"Ask Mong about it," NgGung said. He turned to walk away.

"Wait," Seh said. "Why did you stare at me like that when you mentioned Tonglong?"

NgGung glanced back and stroked his long, thin mustache with a dirty hand. "I just realized how much you look like Tonglong. The two of you could pass for brothers."

Tonglong eased his stallion alongside a large hole in the rocky ground and dismounted. Sweat ran in shimmering streams down the horse's thick black neck, glistening in the rays of the rising sun. The horse had been ridden hard all night and began to shiver, though not from exhaustion or cold.

Tonglong slipped his long ponytail braid into the red silk sash around his green robe. He knelt down, peering into the hole. Inside, a stone-lined cavity opened into an underground space big enough to fit several grown men. But no man in his right mind would attempt to enter there now. Coiled loosely below was a gigantic snake as long as three men were tall.

Tonglong felt a rare smile form on his face. The

snake had grown considerably since the last time he'd seen it. He stood and untied a large cloth bag from his saddle, holding it at arm's length. As he set it on the ground, a drop of reddish brown liquid fell from the bag's stained bottom into the hole. The snake began to stir. It raised its enormous head and flicked out its huge forked tongue, collecting the scent of the fresh kill above, as well as the intruder.

"Welcome, ssstranger," a soft voice hissed from behind Tonglong. "I sssee you bear gifts."

Tonglong spun around and saw a small, hooded figure rise from behind a pile of stones. His smile grew. "Of course," he said. "It would have been rude of me to arrive empty-handed. I wouldn't want to disappoint you, or your friend." Tonglong nodded toward the pit.

The figure drifted forward. "I've never known you to disappoint me, or my friend. You are always ssso generous. I wasn't expecting you for a few more days. How is everything?"

"Everything is perfect," Tonglong replied.

"Then we are on ssschedule?"

"Ahead of schedule, actually," Tonglong said. "And I'd like to keep it that way. You know how much I hate to waste time."

"I do indeed. In that regard, you are just like your father."

Tonglong frowned.

The figure paused. "I'm sssorry to have brought that up. Why don't you give me my present? What is it you brought this time?"

"A little something that was meant for the Emperor, but I would feel much better if it were in your hands." Tonglong motioned toward the bag. "Go ahead, open it."

The figure knelt down and reached a tiny hand into the bag, feeling around. "Is this what I think it is?"

Tonglong nodded.

"What a thoughtful gift! You really shouldn't have. This is going to cost you dearly, you know."

Tonglong shrugged. "You're worth it."

The hooded figure bowed. "Thank you ever so much. I know just what I'll do with it."

The figure pulled Grandmaster's severed head out of the bag and dropped it into the pit.

25

CHAPTER

3

The sun had barely risen above the horizon when Seh stopped at a wide bend in the trail NgGung had told him to follow. Seh hadn't slept all night, and he had been through a lot of stress since the attack. His normally strong connections with the world around him were growing fuzzy. He had to be careful. Seh focused his attention beyond the bend and, sure enough, the pit of his stomach began to tingle. There were several people ahead.

Seh decided to find out who they were before he made his presence known. He stepped off the road into a thick stand of pine trees and looked down at his new blue silk robe. Seh shook his head. Why couldn't it be green?

He pulled the silly merchant's hat onto his head and slipped through the trees toward the opposite side of the bend. Seh followed a carpet of damp pine needles in slow, smooth strides. He took his time, keeping his heart rate low and his *chi* masked. Eventually, he heard a voice. It was definitely a bandit.

"That's not how you do it, you big oaf. Watch me. We didn't go through the trouble of stealing all this gold just so you could leave it scattered all over the road. *This* is how you tie down a tarp—"

Seh was about to introduce himself when he realized that just because the man was a bandit didn't mean that he was one of *Mong's* bandits. Seh needed to be sure. He took a cautious step forward and the hat snagged on a low tree limb, tumbling off his bald head. He had forgotten all about it.

"Hey, did you hear something?" the bandit asked.

Seh didn't wait for the response. He picked up the hat and raced silently back the way he had come. He would wait and try approaching the bandits from a different direction. He was nearly to the road when a huge forearm draped in red silk flew out from behind a tree.

The arm caught Seh square in the chest, and he had to grab the gigantic arm to keep from falling to the ground.

Seh expected the arm to drop under his weight, but it didn't. It held firm, parallel to the ground, and Seh found himself hanging from it like a tree snake dangling from a mighty oak.

"You should watch where you're going," Mong said as he stepped out from behind the tree. "You never know what you might bump into." Mong shook his huge arm, and Seh lost his grip, dropping to the ground. He landed on his knees.

"Be more careful out here," Mong said as he adjusted his enormous red silk robe. His thick neck and shoulder muscles rippled beneath it. "Ours is a dangerous business. If that had been a sword instead of my arm, we wouldn't be having this conversation right now. Do you understand?"

Seh nodded. He could have kicked himself for getting caught—by Mong, no less.

"Good," Mong said. "Now, what are you doing here?"

Seh felt his face begin to flush. "Ying came back to Cangzhen. With *qiang*s. The temple has been destroyed."

"I see," Mong said. He looked Seh up and down. "I recognize that outfit as NgGung's. Is that how you found us?"

Seh nodded.

"NgGung does not give up his secrets easily," Mong said. "And I've never known him to give up his clothes. I'm impressed."

Seh shrugged.

Mong cleared his throat. "It's good that you escaped, Seh, and that you came looking for me. Did Grandmaster make it out alive?"

"I don't know," Seh said.

"I can see why NgGung shared my whereabouts,"

Mong said. "If Grandmaster is dead, that would be very, very bad. Grandmaster is the glue that keeps the fragile pieces of this region together." Mong shook his huge, bald head. "Did any of your brothers survive? The youngest among you, I mean."

"Grandmaster saved all of us," Seh replied. "He hid me, Fu, Malao, Hok, and Long. Why would he do that?"

"I'm sure Grandmaster had his reasons," Mong said. "I will not speculate on his motivations."

Seh's jaw tightened. "I remember one time you visited and asked Grandmaster if my brothers and I were 'ready.' Ready for what?"

Mong paused. "Cangzhen meant everything to Grandmaster. He knew he was growing old, and he knew Cangzhen was at risk because of the shifting politics in this region and throughout China. He wanted to ensure Cangzhen's survival. To do that, he needed a successor. Ideally, several successors who would complement each other and keep Cangzhen a dynamic place. You five were to be Cangzhen's future."

"But . . . why us?" Seh asked.

"You are all the offspring of powerful warriors," Mong said, "and fate planted the five of you on his doorstep at roughly the same time. Grandmaster took that to be a sign. You are my son and have inherited many of the same skills. Fu is the son of a great tiger-style kung fu master named Sanfu. The list goes on."

"*Sanfu* is Cantonese for 'Mountain Tiger,'" Seh said. "Was Fu's father a Cangzhen monk—*like you*?"

Mong's pale forehead wrinkled. "I see you got

more information out of NgGung than just my where-abouts. Good for you. Yes, Sanfu was a Cangzhen war-rior monk—just like me."

"Who is Tonglong, then?" Seh asked.

"Tonglong is one of the Emperor's top soldiers," Mong said. "But he has nothing to do with Cangzhen. I do not know why he has a Cantonese insect name. Why do you ask?"

"NgGung told me to tell you that he saw Tonglong with Ying yesterday."

"What?" Mong said, folding his enormous arms. "Did you ask NgGung if he told anybody?"

Seh nodded. "He said he told Grandmaster."

"*Before* the attack?"

"Yes."

"Did NgGung say anything else?" Mong asked.

"He suggested somebody warn the monks at Shaolin Temple."

Mong stared at Seh. "That's a very good idea. *Someone* should warn them."

"Me?" Seh asked.

"I can't think of anyone better," Mong said. He unfolded his arms and placed a hand on Seh's shoul-der. "I need every one of my men to help transport our shipment back to the stronghold. You are young, fast, and silent. You are also intelligent and resource-ful. You could get there without Ying finding out."

Seh stared at Mong, unsure how to respond. Mong had just given him more compliments in a few sen-tences than he had given him his entire life.

Mong slapped Seh on the back. "I'll give you directions to Shaolin. It should take you about ten days if you travel only at night, which is what I suggest. Spend a day or two at Shaolin. The monks there are good people. After that, join us at the stronghold."

Seh nodded. He wasn't sure how he felt about joining a bandit gang, but at least it meant he might be able to get the bandits to help him.

"You look like you could use some rest," Mong said. "Spend the day with us, sleeping atop one of the carts. We eat our main meal just before sunset. You can leave after that. Remind me to give you directions to the stronghold, too, so that you can find us later. I should warn you, though, as you did with NgGung, you may have to fight my men to see me."

"I'm not afraid," Seh said.

Mong smiled. "Good. We should get moving, then. Why don't we—"

Mong suddenly straightened and snapped his head in the direction of the trail.

Seh felt it, too. The pit of his stomach began to tingle. A little at first, then more and more until it seemed a thousand ants were crawling beneath his belly button. He had experienced this same sensation only one other time—while hiding in the water barrel during the attack on Cangzhen.

"Soldiers are coming," Seh whispered.

"Not soldiers," Mong corrected. "Monkeys."

CHAPTER
4

"I'll never understand monkeys," Seh mumbled to himself as he pushed forward alone, into the darkness.

It had been more than twelve hours since the monkey troop had attacked, and Seh was still finding it hard to believe that Malao had been with the monkeys. Malao's actions to save the monkeys from the bandits' swords and spears had been crazy, but remarkable. Even more amazing had been Malao's fight with Hung, the enormous bear-style kung fu master who was Mong's right-hand man. Malao may be small, but he was tough. Seh had tracked Malao down less than an hour ago, and Malao had come away from his battle with Hung without a scratch.

Seh rubbed his sweaty, stubbly-haired head as he

thought about the new information Malao had given him. Grandmaster was dead, Fu had somehow managed to obtain the dragon scrolls Ying was after, and Hok was at Cangzhen keeping an eye on Ying and, presumably, Tonglong.

Malao was going to rendezvous with Hok tomorrow, and he had invited Seh to join them. Seh had several reasons he'd like to accept the offer, but he had already concluded that it would be best if he went directly to Shaolin Temple. Seh realized that while it would be good to try and get the bandits to help him and his brothers, the monks of Shaolin Temple would be even better allies. They were stronger and far more respectable than a gang of bandits ever would be.

Then again, maybe he should try and get the bandits *and* the Shaolin monks to help?

Enough! Seh muttered to himself. It was time to give his brain a rest. He slowed to a fast walk and began to push the items in his mind out one at a time. It was a walking meditation exercise he'd learned at Cangzhen. The more he pushed out, the more he slowed down. By the time the sun began to rise on the second day of his journey, Seh was sound asleep in a fern grove with an empty head.

Seh slept most of the day away and woke with only a few hours of sunlight left. Though he was hungry, he spent the remaining daylight sitting next to a small stream, meditating more. His connection with the world had been strained by recent events. He needed to try and reestablish the harmony he normally felt with the world around him. Not just harmony with other people, but harmony with all living things.

Seh sat with his eyes closed on a small patch of sand next to the stream, letting the endless ripples of sound wash every thought from his mind. His breathing was smooth . . . controlled. Slowly he began to feel alive again. Once more, he felt the energy of life all around him, flowing freely from one creature to the next. And he was part of it. *Chi* circulated through his body and through the birds in the trees and through the very trees themselves.

Alone, Seh was one with the universe. But when others were around, he became distracted. The only person Seh could be around and still maintain a perfect connection was Hok. And sometimes when they were alone, Seh would feel even more connected.

As Hok drifted into Seh's mind, he opened his eyes. Not surprisingly, he saw a crane standing on the bank downstream.

Seh watched it closely. It was hunting. Oddly enough, the crane's attention was not focused on the water, but on land. Its eyes were glued to a snake.

From where he sat, Seh could see that the reptile was a young beauty snake, about as long as his arm. Beauty snakes were not poisonous. They had three vibrant, distinctly different color patterns on their bodies that often made them look like three completely different snakes spliced together. This one was no exception. Most of the top half was a brilliant green, and the bottom half was solid black. A yellow stripe began at the back of its head and ran down its spine all the way to the tip of its tail. Stranger still was its head. The entire thing was bright blue—almost the same color as Seh's silk robe—and there was a thick black stripe across each eye.

Seh had never seen a snake that strange or that beautiful. He was considering taking a closer look when the crane struck.

The white head of the crane shot toward the snake with astonishing speed. To Seh's surprise—and relief—the snake sent a powerful ripple through its muscular torso, slithering out of the path of the crane's deadly beak.

The snake slithered off toward the forest. Again the crane thrust its beak at the snake, and again the snake sent a pulse along its spine.

Seh grinned, but only for a moment, as the crane hopped forward and came down over the snake. One of the crane's razor-sharp claws dug deep into the beauty snake's yellow stripe. At the same time, the snake thrust its head up and back, connecting with one of the crane's thighs.

The crane squawked and Seh jumped to his feet, heading toward the battle. He saw the crane release the snake and hop backward. It puffed out its chest and fanned its wings powerfully as the snake rose up, poised to strike again.

"Get out of here!" Seh shouted at the crane.

The crane looked at Seh and flew off. Seh saw a line of red running across its downy thigh.

The snake lay in a loose pile, bright red blood oozing out between green, yellow, and black scales.

Seh cautiously reached down to it. The snake remained limp as he gently stroked its back.

Quickly, Seh removed his hat and tore out the inner silk lining. He bound the snake's wounds with the silk and placed the snake inside the hat. The snake seemed slightly more alert, which was a good sign. Still, it didn't try to escape, even after Seh washed his hands, picked up the hat, and headed into the forest toward Shaolin.

For several days, Seh's routine was the same. He traveled all night, slept all day, and spent the time between searching for food, meditating, and tending the snake. Some of the nights were filled with heavy rain, while others were perfectly clear. It didn't matter to Seh. He accepted whatever came.

Mong had given him a route that went over numerous small, steep mountains instead of around them. It was exhausting travel, but Seh welcomed the exercise.

As the days passed, Seh noticed two significant changes. First, the snake's condition improved dramatically. It began spending most of its time on Seh's left arm. The snake seemed to enjoy resting its head on the warm pulse of Seh's wrist, the remainder of its body coiled around his arm beneath his long silk sleeve.

Seh tried letting it go several times after he

removed its bandages, but every time he set it down, the snake would immediately crawl up his leg, around his slender waist and chest, over his shoulder, and down his arm. Since the snake tended to do this *beneath* his clothes, Seh soon stopped trying to release it and just let it tag along. He figured when the snake was hungry enough, it would leave.

The second change came within Seh himself. Or rather, without. It was his hair.

Ever since Seh could remember, his hair had grown faster than everyone else's. Most of the Cangzhen monks shaved their heads every four or five days, but Seh had to shave his every day. If he waited any longer, his hair would grow back quickly and unevenly, making his head look lopsided. Everyone used to make fun of him, except for Hok, who would shave her head as often as he did to make him feel better.

Seh's black hair was now longer than it had ever been and so thick that his hat wouldn't fit—even without the lining. Seh was trying to decide where to dispose of his hat one morning when he noticed a peculiar, smoky smell. He glanced up at the low surrounding mountains and realized it was probably Shaolin Temple. Seh followed his nose.

As the sun rose above the trees, Seh stepped to the edge of a strange clearing. More than two hundred stone monuments of various shapes and sizes reached toward the sky. He grinned. He was standing at the edge of Shaolin's famous Pagoda Forest. The Shaolin Temple compound must be nearby.

Seh began to weave through the pagodas, but after a few steps, he froze. Something was wrong. He reached out around him with all his senses and noticed . . . nothing. The area felt dead. He didn't even sense wildlife. He thought it might be the fact that he was standing in the middle of what was essentially a cemetery, but then he lifted his eyes toward the far end of the pagodas. In the hazy morning light, he saw smoke. Too much smoke.

Seh began to run. The wind in his face brought stronger and stronger scents of smoldering wood and rotting flesh. He reached the main gates of the Shaolin compound and stopped in his tracks.

Bloated bodies were stacked five high in neat rows near the temple's open gates. Orange-robed monks with holes in their chests lay piled alongside armor-clad soldiers with splintered spears and broken swords protruding from their necks and armpits. Half-dry riverbeds of crimson crisscrossed the ground in every direction. Seh fought the urge to retch as the smoky, putrid air circulated through his lungs and swarms of flies buzzed around his head.

Seh didn't know what to do. These were Shaolin warrior monks—the best fighters in all of China. What had brought about this devastation? Who was responsible? It couldn't have been Ying. This attack was at least a couple of days old. Ying would never have been able to travel this far that fast with troops.

Seh looked over at the compound walls. Near the gates, large sections were crumbling away. It looked as though an angry dragon had smashed them with its mighty tail. He glanced around and saw a line of what appeared to be gigantic *qiang*s. The hollow end of each was huge—almost as big as his head. Seh realized they must have caused the damage. Those weapons would make their owner enormously powerful. Whoever owned them certainly wouldn't leave them here. He would return to collect them. Seh decided he needed to hide.

He took a deep breath, trying not to choke on the stench, and hurried back the way he had come. He quickly located a large oak near the edge of the Pagoda Forest and shimmied up it. High above the ground, the air seemed clearer. Seh breathed deeply, over and over, until he felt life circulating through him once more. He remained there for the better part of the day, occasionally reaching out with his senses for some sign of life other than the snake around his wrist. Once darkness fell, he would head for the bandit stronghold to report the unbelievable news. Until then, he would wait.

It was late afternoon when the pit of Seh's stomach began to tingle. Oddly enough, the snake around his arm shivered at exactly the same moment. They both sensed the presence of an intruder. Or, more precisely, two intruders. If Seh hadn't known better, he would have thought it was a monkey and a tiger. But he knew monkeys and tigers never traveled together. He listened closely and soon heard familiar voices arguing. It was Malao and Fu.

Seh cast his focus in every direction. He hoped to hear Hok's quiet voice or sense her smooth, calm presence, but didn't hear or feel anything remotely calm.

Seh sighed and slipped down the tree. At least Malao and Fu might have some information for him. And, as frustrating as they might be sometimes, it would be good to see them again.

As Seh approached, he heard Fu announce that he was going to the temple. Seh watched as Fu headed off and was about to follow, but something made him stop. He sensed a large amount of feline *chi* coming from Fu's direction. Even the snake sensed it and shivered.

If Fu was emitting that much *chi*, he was bound to be feisty. Seh decided to let him go.

Seh should have paid closer attention to his gut— and to the snake. If he had concentrated harder, he might have realized that the additional *chi* was actually coming from a second feline kung fu master on the prowl. He might even have sensed the dragon that was about to swoop in like an eagle or the praying mantis that was patiently watching everyone and everything.

"Can you hear me, Major Ying?" Tonglong asked. "Are you all right?"

Ying could hardly make out Tonglong's words. Ying was barely conscious, flat on his back among the trees beside Shaolin's Pagoda Forest. The grooves in his face were caked with dirt and sweat, and his robe was peeled open across his chest. His green tattooed eyelids were half closed.

"*Listen closely, if you can,*" Tonglong said, kneeling over Ying. "*General Tsung, the renegade leopard-style master from Shaolin, rendered you unconscious with an unorthodox choke hold. I have since subdued him. The boys now have the dragon scrolls and . . .*"

Ying felt himself slipping away again. Trying to stay

awake, he focused on the first thing he saw—Tonglong's straight sword. The long, flawless blade glimmered in the late-afternoon light, and Ying's mind began to wander. A forgotten chamber in the back of his mind opened. In it were secrets from his past. Secrets that centered on another sword—Grandmaster's dragon sword.

Grandmaster's straight sword was generations old and responsible for a thousand deaths. It was almost as famous as Grandmaster himself. Grandmaster was now dead, and he would eventually be forgotten. But the sword . . . it, too, must be destroyed, just like the five pampered children chosen to carry Cangzhen's torch.

His mind still adrift, Ying thought back to the first time he had seen Grandmaster—and the dragon sword.

A three-year-old boy was playing with a long rope in the center of a bustling mountain camp. It was almost lunchtime, and a woman called out, "Saulong, *sic fan*! Time to eat!"

Saulong responded to his mother's call immediately. He was hungry. He raced to his family's elaborate tent, making sure he removed his sandals before stepping onto the thick animal skins that blanketed the ground inside.

"Leave your whip outside, Saulong," his mother said. "You know the rules—only your father can bring his weapon into our home."

Saulong smiled. He knew his whip was only a piece of rope, but it pleased him that his mother saw it as equal to his father's metal chain whip.

As Saulong dropped his rope and stepped inside, he heard a pain-filled scream. He spun around and peered out the tent's entrance. A few steps from where he had been playing, Saulong saw a stranger. It was a man old enough to be his grandfather, carrying a straight sword. The blade was decorated with intertwining dragons. Bright red liquid dripped off the tip.

Saulong looked behind the stranger and saw Han, the blacksmith, flopping about on the ground. Han was trying desperately to push his insides back into a large slice across his midsection. Saulong shivered but continued to stare.

"Cholong—*Loud Dragon!*" the old stranger called out in Cantonese. "Come face your destiny!"

Saulong's eyes widened. Cholong was his father's name! What did this stranger want with his father?

"Saulong!" his mother whispered sharply. "Get away from the door!"

"No," Saulong replied. "I want to watch."

"Ugh!" his mother said. "There is no doubt you are your father's son. Watch, then, and learn the ways of your ancestors."

Saulong's mother began to stuff things into a bag while Saulong kept his eyes glued to the stranger. Within moments, it seemed every man in camp had surrounded the old man. Twenty men armed with spears and swords attacked the stranger as one.

It was over almost as soon as it began. From what Saulong saw, the stranger did nothing more than whirl his sword a few times, but nearly every man from the camp had fallen to it. The three men that were still breathing ran off.

Saulong could hardly believe his eyes. He had seen men fight before, but the men would only use their fists, and the fights never ended like this. The men on the ground all seemed to be . . . dead. Like a rabbit or pig before cooking.

"Nice work, old man," a deep voice said in the distance. "I assume you're warmed up now."

Saulong grew nervous. That was his father's voice. His father approached from the edge of camp, leading a horse.

"I found this beast tethered outside my camp," Cholong said to the stranger. "I recognized it as yours. I'm impressed this old mare is still useful."

"Some things improve with age," the old man replied.

Cholong laughed. "We shall see about that." He pulled his long metal chain whip from his sash and began to swing it. "I'm a bit more of a challenge than my men."

The stranger didn't respond.

"Any last words?" Cholong asked.

The stranger remained silent.

Cholong hissed like a dragon and spat on the ground. "I've waited most of my life for this, old man. If you don't want to talk, let's just finish it."

And with that, Cholong attacked. He and the stranger exchanged blows so quickly, Saulong could not follow everything. What he did see clearly, though, was his father's chain whip wrap around the stranger's sword. As his father gripped his chain with both hands and wrenched the sword free of the stranger, the stranger lashed out with a dragon fist.

The fist struck Cholong square in the face, and he crumpled to the ground. His body jerked twice, then fell still.

"NO!" Saulong cried.

The stranger looked at Saulong, expressionless, then turned his attention back to Cholong.

"Saulong!" his mother whispered. "Turn around!"

But Saulong didn't budge. He watched the stranger bend over and remove four scrolls from the folds of Cholong's luxurious red robe.

Saulong's mother grabbed his shoulder and spun him around. She was holding a small pack. She looked him in the eye. "We must RUN!"

Saulong's mother bolted from the tent. Saulong followed as fast as his little legs could carry him. "MaMa!" Saulong cried, racing after her. Tears streamed sideways across his face. He'd made less than a dozen strides when someone grabbed the back of his robe and yanked him to a stop.

Saulong jerked his head around and saw the old stranger.

"You are coming with me, child," the man said in a firm voice.

"No!" Saulong screamed. He looked into the trees and saw his mother stop. She glanced first at him, then at the old stranger. The stranger raised his dragon sword and shook his head.

"NO!" Saulong said again.

Saulong's mother looked back at him. He saw tears falling from her eyes. "Never forget me," she said in a shaky voice. "And never forget your name."

And then she was gone.

Saulong let out a hate-filled cry and tore free of the old man's grip. He ran to his family's tent and grabbed his rope whip, then ran even faster back to face the stranger. Saulong lashed out at the man's legs, arms, and face, and the stranger stood perfectly still, silently accepting the beating. When Saulong's right arm grew tired, he switched the rope to his left. When his left arm grew tired, he began to kick. And when his legs finally gave out, the old man lifted him up and carried him to the horse. The stranger climbed on, and off they went.

As they raced down the mountain, Saulong whispered to himself over and over, *Never forget my mother, never forget my name. . . .*

Saulong—*Vengeful Dragon*. The three-year-old didn't know what *vengeful* meant, but he would learn.

CHAPTER
6

Seh found himself running through the forest again. This time, he wasn't alone.

"Slow down, Seh," Malao said from the treetops. "Give Fu a chance to catch up."

Seh slowed to a stop and stared up at Malao, silhouetted in the evening sun. They had been running from Shaolin and the fight between Ying and the Emperor's leopard-style master, General Tsung, for less than an hour.

"Don't tell me Fu has fallen behind already," Seh said. "Where is he?"

"How should I know?" Malao replied. He grabbed a thick vine and began to climb down. "You're the one with the creepy ability to sense other people. I only realized Fu wasn't behind us anymore because I haven't heard him complaining in a while."

Seh frowned. As he waited for Malao, he slipped one hand inside the folds of his robe. The three dragon scrolls he'd swiped from Tsung were still there. The snake on his wrist crawled higher up his sleeve, out of sight.

"Should we go back and look for Pussycat?" Malao asked as he released the vine high in the air. He tucked into a tight somersault and landed in front of Seh, still talking. "Or do you think Fu will sniff us out?"

"He'll sniff us out for sure," Seh said, wrinkling his nose. "When was the last time you washed your feet? They stink."

Malao looked down and wiggled his dark-skinned toes. He giggled.

Seh shook his head. "Climb back up there and keep an eye out for Fu. Keep an eye out for Ying, too."

"Ying?" Malao said. "He won't be bothering us anytime soon. Did you see the way that guy Tsung took him down? I've never seen a hold like that."

"Yes, Malao, I saw it," Seh said. "Now please get up there."

"Oh, no," Malao said, folding his arms. "I'm not going anywhere until you answer some questions."

"We don't have time for games," Seh said.

"This isn't a game," Malao replied. "I want to know what's going on."

Seh glanced about. "I have no idea what you're talking about."

"Come on, Seh," Malao said. "Tsung talked about Hok being a girl. Fu and I had no idea, but you did. How long have you known?"

"Long enough," Seh replied.

"How come you never told us?"

Seh shrugged. "It was none of your business."

"None of our business?" Malao said. "Hok is our brother! I mean . . . sister. How could you keep that a secret?"

"If Hok wanted you to know that she was a she, she would have told you. I found out by accident."

"What kind of accident?" Malao asked. "What other secrets are you hiding?"

"None."

"I don't believe you. What's going on with Tonglong?"

"Tonglong?" Seh said. "Nothing. I don't know anything about him. Do you?"

"I know that he looks just like you," Malao said. "And that he winked at me back at Shaolin."

"He *winked* at you?"

"Yes," Malao said. "Right after he took the fourth dragon scroll from Ying."

"Tonglong took a dragon scroll from Ying?" Seh asked. "Are you sure?"

"Positive," Malao said. "You still have the other three, don't you?"

"Yes," Seh said. He patted the folds of his robe and his sleeve slid up toward his elbow. The beauty snake's brilliant blue head poked out.

"Hey!" Malao said. "What's that? Another secret?"

"It's just a snake," Seh said. "It was wounded, and I helped it. It likes hanging around, and I can't seem to get rid of it."

"Oh," Malao said. He looked into the trees. "I wish my friend the white monkey was around. I haven't seen it since it led me and Fu to Shaolin."

"Would that be the same white monkey I saw with the monkey troop?" Seh asked. "The group that attacked the bandits?"

"That's right," said Malao. He scowled. "Those bandits are mean."

"You'd better get used to them," Seh said. "I'm trying to get them to help us. I had hoped to get the Shaolin monks to help us, too, but that's no longer an option, unfortunately."

Malao suddenly grew quiet and lowered his head. Seh thought he saw tears welling in Malao's eyes. "Seh, do you think what Tsung said about Hok is true? Do you think that she really . . . you know . . . *died* during the attack?"

Seh patted Malao's fuzzy head. "I don't know what to think. If anyone can take care of herself, though, it's Hok. You know that."

Malao sniffled. "I guess you're right. So, you don't know anything about this guy Tonglong?"

"No," Seh replied. "He is the biggest mystery. I didn't get a clear view of his face back at Shaolin Temple, but his *chi* felt strangely familiar. Still, I'm certain I've never met him before. I don't know what to make of it."

"Me either," Malao said. "So, what are we going to do next?"

"I was thinking we should—" The snake on Seh's arm suddenly shivered and retracted its head beneath Seh's sleeve.

Malao looked at Seh. "What's wrong with him?"

"Shhh," Seh said. "Someone's coming."

A moment later, Fu burst through a tangle of bushes, panting heavily.

"Pussycat!" Malao said. "It's about time you showed up."

Fu growled. "I heard you two . . . talking . . . about where we're going . . . next. Tell me."

"We're going to the bandit stronghold," Seh announced.

"What!" Malao squeaked. "You never said anything about that! No way! Hung will kill me. And then he'll eat me!"

Malao slid one hand inside the folds of his robe. Seh saw that Malao was carrying his carved monkey stick.

"No one will harm you as long as you're with me, little brother," Seh said.

"No," Malao said. "No, no, NO!"

Fu looked at Malao. "Are these the same bandits you told me about?"

Malao nodded.

"I don't know, Seh," Fu said. "I know some people who might be able to help. The governor of this region—"

Seh raised a hand. "This isn't up for discussion. We're going to the stronghold."

Fu locked eyes with Seh. "Since when did you become the leader?"

"Do you know how to find the Governor?" Seh asked.

Fu didn't reply.

"There you go," Seh said. He looked at Malao. "What about you? Do you know how to get anywhere from here?"

Malao looked at the ground.

Seh straightened up. "Mong, the bandit leader, gave me detailed directions to his stronghold. Like it or not, we need their help. So that's where I'm going. You two can follow me, or you can wander around together until Ying catches up with you. It's your choice. I'm done talking."

"Fine," Malao said. He looked at Fu. "Maybe we're done talking to you, too. And maybe we'll follow you, but we won't talk to you. Not a single word. Right, Fu?"

Fu nodded.

"Oh, grow up," Seh said.

Malao clamped his hands over his mouth.

Seh laughed. "I could only be so lucky." He shook his head and began the long walk toward the bandit stronghold.

More than a week later, Seh's luck was still holding out. Like before, he traveled at night and slept during the day. Malao and Fu did the same, following in Seh's tracks, sometimes as much as a *li* behind. Seh occasionally heard a distant complaint from Fu or a giggle from Malao, but he only joined them when he saw the thin tendrils of smoke from the cooking fires Malao made at daybreak with his fire stone. Soon after eating the mushrooms and other items Malao had picked along the way, Seh would head off alone with the snake. The snake would uncurl itself from his arm and disappear to hunt or poke around on its own, and Seh would meditate, then sleep.

Malao and Fu had remained true to their word and hadn't talked to him the entire time. They talked to each other, though, and Seh sensed that something had changed in both of them. Maybe they *were* growing up.

Seh decided it was time to say something to Malao and Fu. He wouldn't admit it to them, but he was beginning to feel left out and a little lonely. He decided mealtime would be the best time to do it.

But as luck would have it, the pit of Seh's stomach began to tingle well before there was any sign of a campfire.

CHAPTER 7

"Halt! Who goes there?"

Seh stepped out from behind a large elm tree onto a wide, well-worn trail. In the early-morning half light, he saw a man with a spear. Seh stood still and the snake slithered up his arm, out of sight.

Seh stared hard at the man. He knew he was close to the stronghold. The man was probably a guard. Mong had told him to be firm with the perimeter guards and not show weakness. Mong had also said if he needed to provoke the guards for any reason, all he had to do was call them peasants. They hated being called peasants.

Seh's fine silk robe was no longer in perfect condition, but it still looked much nicer than the simple cotton robe this man was wearing. Seh reached into his robe and pushed the scrolls around his body, then tightened the sash so that the scrolls were secured in the small of his back. If he had to fight, the scrolls wouldn't get in the way.

Seh cleared his throat like he had seen some of Grandmaster's wealthier guests do. "My name is Seh," he said. "I've come to see Mong."

The spearman shook his balding head. "Your name is 'snake' and you're looking for someone named 'python'? What do I look like, a zookeeper? Be on your way."

Seh didn't move.

"I said, *be on your way*," the man repeated.

Seh folded his arms. "I know your game, and I'm prepared to fight for information. *One new thing you'll know for every solid blow*, right?"

"What are you talking about?" the man said. "The only fighting I do is *to the death*. Everything else is child's play. You do not want to cross hands with me, boy."

Seh smirked. This man was too arrogant. It had been Seh's experience that people who boast of their skill have little. Seh took a step closer. "Tell me how to find Mong."

The man raised his spear. "I don't know anyone named Mong."

Seh stared deep into the spearman's eyes. The man's pupils narrowed and his eyes darted to one side. The man was lying.

Seh approached the man.

The guard raised his spear higher and shook it. "Don't make me use this!"

Seh found it amusing that he was being threatened with a spear. Everyone at Cangzhen had learned to use a spear, but no monk of any age could match Seh's skill with the weapon. He was an expert at using one as well as taking one out of the hands of an opponent. If he could provoke the man to attack, Seh thought he could disarm him. Perhaps then the man would be more cooperative.

"Why don't you give that to me?" Seh said, pointing at the spear. "I wouldn't want you to hurt yourself."

The man scowled.

"Well?" Seh said.

The man hesitated.

Seh scoffed and waved his hand, turning away. "Cowardly peasant."

"Who are you calling a peasant!" the man shouted. He thrust his spear at the back of Seh's neck.

Seh sensed the spearman move and heard a subtle *whoosh* of air. He tilted to one side and the spear tip passed harmlessly over his shoulder. Seh grabbed the spear shaft with both hands and lunged forward, pulling the spearman off balance. The man hung on tight with his arms extended, and Seh kicked straight backward. He connected solidly with the spearman's armpit.

The spearman howled and released the weapon, staggering away from Seh. The snake on Seh's arm shivered, and Seh saw two more men running down the trail toward them. One carried a broadsword, the other a bow with an arrow already nocked. They stopped next to the disarmed spearman.

"I do not wish to fight," Seh said, dropping the spear. "I only want to talk to Mong. My name is Seh."

"I don't care what your name is," the swordsman said. "No one talks to Mong. I suggest you turn around and go back the way you came."

Seh shook his head.

"I'm sorry," the swordsman said, stepping toward Seh. "Perhaps you didn't understand what I just said. Maybe I should ask my broadsword to explain it to you? People never seem to misunderstand it."

Seh bent down and picked up the spear. He glanced disapprovingly at the heavy gray robes worn by the guards. "Broadswords are peasant weapons," Seh said. "I don't speak peasant, so I doubt I would understand *it* any better than I do *you*."

The swordsman's face flushed. "You shall pay dearly for that!" He rushed toward Seh with his broadsword held high in one hand, his other arm defensively in front of his chest. This man knew how to fight. Seh had to be careful.

Seh gripped the spear at its center balance point with both hands, his lead hand in an overhand grip and his trailing hand in an underhand grip. When the swordsman was within range, Seh raised the spear high and thrust its razor-sharp tip down at an angle toward the man's stomach.

The swordsman stopped short and swung his

broadsword down in front of his body, knocking the spear tip straight down—exactly as Seh had hoped. Seh used the spear tip's downward momentum to help swing the entire spear end over end in a powerful circle. The tail end of the spear struck the swordsman on the ear and the swordsman sank to his knees.

Seh dropped the spear and dove forward, catching the swordsman's throat in the crux of his elbow. Seh began to squeeze.

A moment later, the swordsman went limp.

Seh loosened his grip slightly, his arm still locked around the swordsman's drooping head. Seh noticed the snake was shivering violently on his left bicep. Seh flashed a stern look at the archer and the spearman.

The archer raised his bow and drew his nocked arrow.

"Put your bow away," Seh said. "Your friend's sleep is only temporary. But if I feel threatened, I'll snap his neck like a rotten tree limb."

"Go ahead," the archer replied. "That scoundrel is no friend of mine. His temper is far too short. Our camp would be better off without him."

Seh blinked. He wasn't expecting a response like that. He scanned the morning shadows for something that might help him get out of this situation. He knew he was no match for a man with a drawn bow. Not at that distance.

Next to the archer, the spearman glanced into the trees. The pit of Seh's stomach began to tingle, and he heard a familiar voice.

"Hey! Why don't you pick on somebody your own size?" It was Malao.

The archer glanced up. "Where did you come from?"

Malao began to giggle.

"What's so funny?" the archer asked.

Malao giggled harder and pointed at the man.

The archer's face darkened. He aimed his bow at Malao. "Why, you little mmmpf—"

The archer's remaining words were shoved back into his mouth by Fu's meaty hand. Seh watch as Fu stepped out of the shadows and snapped the archer's head back far enough to throw the man off balance but not break his neck. The spearman's eyes widened, and he backed toward the unconscious swordsman.

Fu tossed the bow, arrow, and quiver into the trees. The archer attempted to stand, but Fu pounced on his chest.

"Don't you EVER point that thing at my little brother," Fu growled in the archer's face. "Do you understand?"

The archer nodded.

Seh took a step toward the spearman, and the pit of his stomach began to tingle again as a spasm ripped through the snake on his arm. Seh spun around, expecting to see Malao behind him on the ground. Instead, he saw a medium-sized man with big brown eyes, a large nose, and strange, droopy ears jump out from behind a bush. The man landed on all fours and raised his head, sniffing the air.

Sniff, sniff, sniff. "Let's see...." *Sniff, sniff.* "A snake, a tiger, and a..." *Sniff, sniff, cough!* "Whew! A monkey? What fun!"

Seh grimaced. "Who are *you*?"

The man stood, grinning, and folded his hands like a Cangzhen monk. "I am Gao. Welcome to the stronghold, my brothers."

"I can't believe we came all the way back here because of a stupid dream," Captain Yue said.

Commander Woo looked up from the morning campfire. "Lower your voice!" he whispered. "Don't criticize Major Ying's decisions or his dreams. You've seen the kind of mood he's been in since we left Shaolin."

Captain Yue yawned and examined the sleeve of his ornate silk robe. "I don't care anymore. I'm thinking about ending this assignment. My uncle—*the Emperor*—promised me adventure and excitement. So far, all we've done is trudge through the forest in a big circle. Now we're back at Cangzhen, right where we started. This is ridiculous."

"Major Ying has his reasons for returning," Commander Woo said. "As Major Ying's third in command, you're in no position to question him. And as his number two, it would be my responsibility to stop you. Besides, where would you go?"

"My uncle's summer palace isn't all that far from here," Captain Yue said. "I'm sure I could find it easily enough. If my leg weren't still injured from that encounter with the Drunkard, I'd be on my way right now."

"You aren't going anywhere," Commander Woo said. "I outrank you and—"

"Oh, please," Captain Yue interrupted. "It's not like you could stop me. Your leg is much worse than mine. Tell me again, how was it that you hurt yours?"

Commander Woo stood on his good leg. "Listen to me, you—"

Ying emerged from the shadows beyond the campfire. "That's enough!" he hissed. He looked at Commander Woo. "You should know better than to argue like this out in the open. What if the men heard you?"

Commander Woo sat down and lowered his head.

Ying looked at Captain Yue and the grooves in his forehead deepened. "I promised your uncle—*the Emperor*—I would personally keep an eye on you. You will go nowhere until I say so. You and Commander Woo had better be ready to strike camp the moment Tonglong arrives."

"Yes, sir," Commander Woo said. "Do you expect

him soon? He's followed the young monks from Shaolin, right?"

"Yes," Ying replied. "I expect he'll meet us here in the next few days. He rode that demon horse of his, which will speed his travel considerably."

Commander Woo nodded.

"One more thing," Ying said. "I need you to find a green tree snake for my drink tonight. The blood from the brown ground dwellers you've been using lately doesn't seem to taste as good with the powdered dragon bone."

"Of course, sir," Commander Woo said. "As you wish."

Ying looked at Captain Yue. Captain Yue was brushing his eyebrows with a tiny jade comb.

Ying shook his head and turned away. "Hopeless!" he muttered, heading across the Cangzhen compound toward Grandmaster's residence. It was time to take care of what had brought him back here. With every step, Ying grew angrier.

"Grandmaster disrespected me," Ying said to himself. "His family and friends will suffer like I have suffered. I will smash his network and hack off every limb of his family tree. I will erase his entire clan as if they never existed."

Enraged, Ying reached the broken gate of Grandmaster's residence and found it hanging by one of its massive hinges. Ying slammed his fists into the gate, splintering it into a thousand pieces.

Ying had always hated Grandmaster's personal

compound. He remembered once asking Grandmaster why a second series of walls was necessary around his residence. Grandmaster responded by making Ying scrub every speck of every wall with a small brush. Cleaning the walls was supposed to give Ying time to "cleanse his mind of trivial interests" that didn't concern him. Instead, it raised more questions. It also made Ying's arms ache. It took him two weeks.

Ying spat on one of the compound walls and trudged into Grandmaster's residence. Early-morning light poured in through several charred holes in the roof, illuminating a single large room with a small bed and a medium-sized table. A few of the walls were blackened, but for the most part the flames hadn't damaged much. Not even the straight sword. Ying saw it hanging on the wall in its scabbard, tip down—a sign of respect for the sword.

Though the scabbard was charred, Ying recognized it immediately. He snatched it off the wall and drew the sword. The blade was covered with an ornate pattern of intertwining dragons. It was without question Grandmaster's. Grandmaster apparently hadn't had time to retrieve it during the attack.

Ying hissed and threw the sword against the wall with all his might. He grabbed the wooden scabbard with both hands spread wide and broke it over his knee. Ying threw the halves down and looked at the sword. The handle was worn, but the blade was in pristine condition. It glimmered majestically in a pool of light on the floor.

It was said that all great swords have souls. Grandmaster's sword looked like a great sword. If it were, Ying would have to kill it. He picked up the sword again. This time, it spoke to him.

Ying's mind flooded with images of both Grandmaster and his father. Happy images as well as sad. Images of both men in life and in death. As he held the sword, Ying was reminded that his father had not fallen to it, but had instead fallen to Grandmaster's dragon fist. But to Ying, it didn't matter. His father had fallen to Grandmaster, and this sword was Grandmaster's—therefore, the sword must be erased from memory just like Grandmaster.

The sword continued to call out to Ying, but he closed his mind to it. He knew what was happening. All the finest swords were made with a special, secret ingredient that gave them not only superior strength, but also a soul. They were forged with blood. The sword maker would slice his arm and cool the blade with his very essence, breathing life into his creation by bonding his own elements with the minerals in the metal. If Grandmaster's ancestors had forged this sword, it was as much a part of Grandmaster's family as any of his human relatives. The sword, like the rest of Grandmaster's relatives, must die.

Ying carried the sword outside and hurled it onto a section of roof that had survived the flames. Exposed to the elements and out of sight from the ground, the sword would wither and decay like a for-gotten man on a mountaintop.

Ying stared at Grandmaster's former residence and raised a fist to the heavens. "I will erase your past like you tried to erase mine, old man! And once I retrieve the dragon scrolls, all of China will know my name! *Saulong*—Vengeful Dragon!"

"Your name is *Dog*?" Seh said, staring at the strange man with the big nose and peculiar floppy ears.

Sniff, sniff. "You bet," Gao replied. "The one and only dog-style master ever to come out of Cangzhen!" Gao dropped back down onto all fours and pretended to chase his tail.

Malao giggled and scurried down the tree. Fu climbed off the archer and glared at the spearman, who was still standing beside the unconscious swordsman.

Malao ran over to Seh, and Fu joined them. Gao sat up. Gao glanced at the other bandits and shook his head. "What a pathetic bunch." He leaned his nose toward one of Malao's tiny footprints. *Sniff, sniff, sniff.*

"Wow, those are some interesting feet you've got there, my friend. You must be Malao."

"Yes!" Malao said. "How did you know?"

"You're famous," Gao said. *Sniff, sniff.* "You defeated Hung. He's Mong's right-hand man, you know. That's no small task, little one, if you'll pardon my pun." He grinned.

Malao laughed. "You're hilarious!"

Sniff. "You think that's funny?" Gao said. "Watch this." He sat back on his haunches and raised one leg all the way up behind one droopy ear. He began to scratch his head with his foot. "Ahhhhh . . ."

Malao laughed and clapped.

Fu rolled his eyes.

Seh watched as Gao rolled over and bounded toward them on all fours. Fu growled, and Seh saw the newly sprouted hairs on the back of Fu's neck stand straight up.

Gao stopped. "What's wrong, my feline friend?" *Sniff, sniff.*

Fu growled again, and Seh placed a hand on Fu's shoulder. "He's just cautious around strangers," Seh said to Gao. "I am, too."

Sniff, sniff. "I can't blame you, especially after what you've been through," Gao said. "I'm really sorry about what happened to Cangzhen."

Seh nodded.

"You're safe now," Gao said. "Mong has been waiting for you. You'll be among friends. Brothers, even. Me, Mong, Hung, and NgGung all grew up at Cangzhen, just like you." *Sniff, sniff.*

Malao's eyes widened, and he punched Seh on the arm. "What do you know about all of this?"

Seh shrugged. "You and Fu chose not to talk to me. What was I supposed to do?"

Sniff, sniff. "Excuse me," Gao said. "I suggest you save the arguing for inside the stronghold. Technically, you're not safe yet. From what I understand, Cangzhen and Shaolin have both been destroyed. Shaolin is about a week's travel from here, but Cangzhen is much closer. We have reports of renewed troop activity at Cangzhen."

"How do you know so much?" Malao asked.

"The bandits have spies," Seh replied. He looked at Gao. "So, you already know about Shaolin?"

Sniff. "Yes. NgGung returned yesterday and brought the news. He also brought news concerning your . . . er . . . brother Hok."

"What do you know about Hok?" Seh asked.

Sniff, sniff, sniff. "I suggest you talk to Mong about that," Gao replied. "It's really none of my business."

Seh's jaw tightened, and Fu growled again.

Sniff. "I'm sorry, but we need to get moving," Gao said. He turned to the archer. "Gather your things and meet us at the shore. Have a torch ready. Hurry!"

The archer nodded and began to scramble.

Gao turned to the spearman. "What are *you* waiting for? Get back to work! Go guard something!"

Woof! Woof! Woof!

"Y-yes, sir!" the spearman said. He grabbed his spear and ran up the trail.

Gao looked at Seh and smiled. "By the way, nice

job disarming that good-for-nothing excuse for a sentry. I appreciate the fact that you didn't skewer him. Good help—or even mediocre help—is so hard to find these days." *Sniff, sniff.*

Seh shrugged.

Gao walked over to the unconscious swordsman and squatted on his haunches. He cradled the back of the man's head in his hands. Seh could tell that Gao was massaging pressure points in the swordsman's neck. It was something all Cangzhen monks learned. A moment later, the swordsman regained consciousness.

The swordsman rubbed his forehead. "Oh . . . I have the worst headache."

Sniff. "You should be ashamed of yourself," Gao said. "You were beaten down by a boy. Take your broadsword and your headache and get back to guarding our stronghold from bloodthirsty soldiers, ruthless thieves, and the occasional child. Go!" *Woof! Woof!*

The swordsman ran off.

Gao's tongue rolled out of his mouth in a sloppy grin and he turned to Malao. He dropped onto all fours. *Pant. Pant. Pant.* "Follow me!" Gao yelped, and sprang down the trail.

"That guy is crazy!" Malao shrieked. "Come on! This is going to be fun!" He also dropped onto all fours and bounded after Gao, dog-style.

Fu looked at Seh. "This can't be happening."

Seh shrugged and motioned down the trail. "After you, Pussycat."

Seh stepped onto a narrow stretch of beach and folded his arms against the crisp morning breeze. The snake around his arm crawled all the way over his shoulder to take shelter among the scrolls in the small of his back.

Seh adjusted his robe and looked west across the wide, circular lake before him. In the center rose a small mountain of jagged rock, sprinkled with patches of evergreen trees. The very top of the mountain was relatively flat and tree-covered. A narrow pathway that Seh took to be stairs ran from the bottom of the small mountain to the plateau at the top.

The stronghold must be up there, Seh thought. It looked impenetrable. Even if invaders were to cross the lake's muddy waters, they would still have to scale the mountain to reach whatever fortress was undoubtedly hidden at the top. It was the perfect stronghold. *How are we going to get over there?* Seh wondered.

"Fire!" Gao barked.

The archer released a flaming arrow toward the mountain island. Seh watched it arc across the morning sky and splash down in the dark water just short of the island.

Malao looked at Gao. "Now what?"

Sniff. "Watch." Gao pointed across the lake.

Seh strained his eyes and saw a long, shallow boat slip into the water from the base of the mountain. A man in gray peasant's clothes climbed aboard and stood at the rear of the boat. He grabbed hold of a single large oar that stretched straight out behind him. The oar was fixed to the boat, and as the boatman began to push it side to side, the boat slowly picked up speed. Soon it was skimming across the water toward them.

Seh's stomach turned. He didn't like water, and he *really* didn't like boats. The snake seemed to sense that Seh was distraught.

Seh glanced around and noticed a collection of low buildings on the northern shore, halfway around the lake. He pointed to them. "What are those buildings?"

Sniff, sniff. "That's our shipyard," Gao replied. "We have several barges that we use to transport goods to and from the stronghold."

Seh looked back at the small craft heading their way. "Why don't we take one of those larger boats instead? I don't think all of us can fit on that small one."

"You'll be fine," Gao said. "We only deploy the bigger boats a few times a year. Besides, most of the boatmen aren't even there right now. They're inside the stronghold helping with a construction project." *Sniff.*

Seh watched the small boat, silent, until the hull scraped against beach sand.

Sniff, sniff. "Time for you to be on your way," Gao said. "I have to leave, too. I need to check on our pitiful excuses for sentries. It was nice meeting all of you—especially the famous bear tamer Malao!"

Malao giggled.

"Wait—" Seh said, but Gao leaped over a row of bushes and disappeared.

The pit of Seh's stomach began to tingle, and the snake shivered. Something wasn't quite right. Seh focused on the boatman as he fussed about the boat. Seh realized what was bothering him. Though there was only one person on board, he sensed *chi* from at least two people—possibly three. That didn't make any sense.

"Let's go!" Malao said. He leaped aboard the boat and sat down.

The boatman ran a callused hand over his short black hair and frowned. "This isn't the most stable craft, young man. I suggest you not make any big movements like that once we're off the beach."

"Sorry," Malao said. "Come on, Fu!"

Fu grumbled and climbed aboard. He sat down and looked at Seh. "Well?"

"Something doesn't feel right," Seh said. "I'm not sure this is such a good idea."

"Oh, don't be like this," Malao said. "You're a snake. All snakes know how to swim. You and your little snake friend will be all right."

"That's not what I'm worried about," Seh said. "I sense something. Something in the water."

Fu looked hard at the boatman. "Is there anything in the water my brothers and I should be worried about?"

"Not at all," the boatman replied. He stepped out of the boat onto the beach.

"See?" Malao said to Seh. "Let's get going. Stop being so paranoid."

Seh sighed. *Perhaps I'm just tired right now,* Seh thought. *Or maybe the water is somehow reflecting the boatman's* chi.

"Come on!" Malao whined.

Seh climbed aboard, and the boatman banged his fist three times against the side of the boat. Seh shot him a suspicious glance.

"For good luck," the boatman said. "We boatmen are a superstitious lot." A large fish rolled farther out in the lake, and the boatman pointed to it. "See?" he said. "A good sign. We'll go now."

The boatman climbed aboard and shoved off, taking his position at the rear of the boat. As the boat began to skim across the muddy water, Seh felt his heart rise up into his throat. His stomach began to turn.

"Wheee!" Malao said. "I've never been on a boat before!"

Seh looked over the side and saw that the boat seemed to be riding dangerously low. He glanced at the boatman.

"We're fine," the boatman said.

"We're better than fine!" Malao said. "Faster! Faster!"

Seh groaned. He sat back and closed his eyes. Between his queasy stomach and Malao's silliness, he didn't think things could get much worse. Halfway across the lake, Seh discovered he was wrong.

"I have to pee," Malao announced.

Seh opened his eyes and looked at Fu.

Fu shook his head. "Put a cork in it until we get to the island, Monkey Boy."

Malao pouted. "I can't."

The boatman cleared his throat. "If you have to go, little one, I suggest you go now. Over the side. We do it all the time. If you wait for the island stronghold, you'll have to use an actual toilet. Mong likes to keep his island clean, so you can't just go anywhere. The closest toilet is way up at the top of the mountain. It's a long walk up there. Believe me."

Malao grinned. "I've never peed in a lake before—"

"Just get it over with," Fu growled.

Malao giggled and stood. He stepped up to the side of the boat, untying his sash. It was a small series of movements, but the boat rocked nonetheless.

"Be careful!" Seh snapped.

Malao giggled again. "This doesn't bother you, does it, big brother?" He began to rock the boat by leaning from side to side. "I guess you're not a water snake—"

"Stop it, Malao," Seh said. He felt sick.

"Hey, look!" Malao replied. "You're turning green! You must be a tree snake. They're almost always green!" He rocked the boat harder.

"STOP IT!" Seh shouted.

Malao stopped. "So sorry," he said, still giggling. Malao tugged at the drawstring on his orange pants and leaned over the side of the boat.

Fu snickered. "You do look pretty funny, Seh. Kind of pale and green and—"

The boat suddenly tilted heavily to one side.

Malao was leaning too far. Without thinking, Seh shifted his weight to the other side to compensate for Malao's mistake. Unfortunately, so did Fu.

The last thing Seh saw as the boat flipped over was Malao somersaulting through the air, laughing hysterically.

Seh hit the water face-first. The force of the flipping boat drove him deep into the murky lake. Long strands of drifting seaweed tangled around his arms, legs, and neck. The snake beneath his robe wriggled up his back but came to a dead end when it reached Seh's collar. It slithered over to Seh's shoulder and clamped nervously around his upper arm, squeezing a major pressure point. Seh felt his arm begin to grow numb.

Seh opened his eyes. They filled with burning, muddy water. He slammed his eyes shut and felt bits of sand and grit grind against his eyeballs.

Seh had no idea which way was up. Blind beneath the water, he picked a direction and started swimming toward it with his one good arm.

Something—someone—grabbed Seh's waist and began to pull him in a different direction.

Seh twisted and turned and thrashed, but it was no use. He felt himself being dragged powerfully through the water. In a last act of defiance, Seh formed a snake-fang fist and raked it across the hands of his attacker.

Seh's attacker released him and shrieked. Seh heard it loud and clear as his head and shoulders exploded out of the water. He opened his eyes and sucked down huge gulps of cool morning air. The snake loosened its grip and managed to poke its head out of the front of Seh's collar.

Seh spun himself around as he began to tread water and saw a girl's head bobbing directly in front of him.

Seh blinked several times. Though she had very short hair, Seh was certain it was a girl. A teenager. It had been her hands on his waist.

Seh realized the girl might very well have just saved his life. She had turned him around and dragged him to the surface. Seh stared at her tiny black eyes, flat face, and smooth, dark skin. She looked just like an eel.

The water exploded behind Seh and he turned to see Fu surface with someone attached to his back.

"Get off me!" Fu roared.

The person on Fu's back released him and kicked away. Seh did a double take. It was a teenage boy with short black hair and a smooth, flat face with dark skin. Like an eel.

The boy dove out of sight.

Seh looked back at the girl and his eyes widened. The boy and girl looked almost identical!

The boy surfaced next to the girl. They smiled at Seh in unison, then disappeared beneath the murky water together.

"Over here!" the boatman called out. He was clinging to the overturned boat. Malao was off to one side, floating happily on his back. Fu was plowing through the water, heading straight for Malao with a scowl on his face.

Seh swam to the boat.

"Who were those two?" Seh asked the boatman as he gripped the side of the upside-down boat.

"Escorts," the boatman replied.

"Were they following us the whole time?" Seh asked. "Underwater?"

The boatman nodded.

"How?"

"They can hold their breath an unnaturally long time," the boatman said. "And when they do need to breathe, they use a small, hollow reed. They can stay underwater for hours."

"They can actually *see* in this water?" Seh asked.

"I'm not sure," the boatman replied. "But I know they can hear really well. Sound travels far underwater."

"*That's* why you banged three times on the side of the boat," Seh said.

The boatman nodded.

"Did one of them signal back by pretending to roll like a fish?"

The boatman grinned. "You are very observant."

Malao squealed, and Seh looked up. Fu had ahold of Malao by the collar and was dunking him repeatedly. Malao erupted with laughter, which seemed to make Fu all the more frustrated.

Seh looked at the boatman. "That girl is a very strong swimmer," Seh said.

"You should see her fight," the boatman said. "Especially in the water. She and her brother are unbeatable together. They fight as one. They might be twins."

Seh glanced over at Fu dunking Malao. "I'm glad they're on our side. I thought she was trying to drown me."

"She could easily have done it," the boatman said. "Lucky for you, things aren't always as they appear at first glance. Especially around here."

Seh nodded. "Where did they go?"

"Who knows? I suspect they see that everything is fine, so they're keeping their distance."

"What are their names?"

"No one knows," the boatman said. "They don't talk. At least, not to us. They seem to communicate with each other, though. We just call them Sum and Cheen."

"Shallow and Deep?" Seh said.

"Yes," the boatman said, frowning. "Just a moment." He turned to Fu and Malao. "Stop playing and save your energy to help us flip this boat."

The boatman looked back at Seh. "Silly children. Now, where was I? Oh, yes—the twins. I think

AnGangseh started calling them that, which would explain why the names are Cantonese. She is from Canton, you know."

"*She?*" Seh said. "*AnGangseh* means 'cobra.' What kind of woman has that for a name?"

"AnGangseh is Mong's wife."

Seh blinked. "Mong is married?"

"Yes," the boatman replied. "Many of the bandits here are married. You'll meet all their wives inside the stronghold."

"Oh . . . ," Seh said. He couldn't help but wonder if AnGangseh was his mother.

"You may be surprised by other things, too," the boatman said. "For instance, there are no children inside the stronghold. As far as I know, you are the first to be allowed inside. Sum and Cheen haven't even been allowed in."

"Really?" Seh asked. "Why not?"

"Mong thinks children are too much trouble to have in the stronghold. He's quite strict about it. If any of the bandits and their wives have a baby, they have to either leave the stronghold or give up their child. I've heard that Mong even gave up his own son."

"I see," Seh said. He turned away from the boatman.

"Excuse me again," the boatman said. He yelled out to Malao and Fu, "That's enough monkey business, you two! Get over here and help us flip this tub upright. We have a lot of bailing to do before she'll float with us in it."

Two hours later, Seh stood alone atop Mong's jagged stone island. He gazed down the longest, narrowest, steepest set of stone stairs he had ever climbed. The stairs had been cut directly into the face of the island mountain. The morning sun had dried the lake water from his blue silk robe, but now it and the scrolls against his back were heavy with sweat from the climb. Fu and Malao were still climbing.

Seh made sure the scrolls and the snake were secure beneath his robe, then he turned and examined the massive gate. It stood taller than three men and was made from entire tree trunks connected side by side. The trees were still covered with bark. From across the lake, the gate blended in with overhanging foliage from trees behind it, giving the illusion of a narrow forest rather than a wide entry. On either side of the gate were sheer stone cliffs that stretched up as high as the gate.

Mong's house, Seh thought. *My father's house. And inside is his wife—possibly my mother. It figures that Mong would have kept her a secret.*

Seh frowned. He wondered what Malao and Fu would think when they learned that he had family behind those gates. He also wondered what his new family members would think of his brothers.

Seh turned to face them.

Malao was looking down at his toes as he climbed. "One thousand fifty-one. One thousand fifty-two. One thousand fifty-three. One thousand—"

Seh looked at Fu's weary face. "Every step?" Seh asked.

Fu growled as he sucked wind. "Every . . . single . . . step. He counted . . . them all. I'm going to . . . kill him."

Fu made it to the narrow ledge in front of the gate and plopped down next to Seh.

"One thousand fifty-five!" Malao said. "Or is it one thousand fifty-six?"

"Please make him stop!" Fu said.

Seh sighed and turned back to the gate. He pounded on it several times. There was hardly a sound. The tree trunks were too thick.

"Let me try," Malao said. He stepped onto the ledge and took a deep breath. "HELLLLLOOOOO!"

The gate began to swing inward.

Malao cleared his throat and looked at Seh. "No need to thank me, big brother." He grinned and stepped up to the opening.

The pit of Seh's stomach began to tingle, and the snake tightened its grip on Seh's arm. "Malao, wait—"

But it was too late. A huge hairy hand yanked Malao into the stronghold, and the gate slammed shut.

CHAPTER
11

Tonglong sat high in a large willow tree, staring westward across the circular lake with the rocky mountain island in the middle. Three tiny black dots had been moving about near the top of the mountain, but their number had just been reduced to two. Soon the remaining two would also disappear, and his job here would be complete.

For now.

Tonglong glanced down the beach from where the young warrior monks had shoved off. He could clearly see two figures—a boy and a girl—sitting side by side, mending a large fishing net. They looked like twins and had hollow sticks dangling from their mouths.

Tonglong thought about how dangerous those hollow tubes could be. For example, if a person were to sink into a murky lake and use one of those tubes to breathe, that person would be at risk of inhaling whatever might happen to pass into that tube. Sleeping mushrooms were plentiful in this region, and it was conceivable that some spores could be drifting about. What if those spores found their way into those hollow sticks? Very dangerous indeed.

Tonglong reached into his robe and pulled out a tube of a different sort—the dragon scroll he had taken from Ying as Ying lay unconscious at Shaolin Temple. He opened it and frowned. It was not the scroll he wanted. The snake boy must have the special one, along with the other two dragon scrolls. Tonglong would have to make plans to acquire them all without arousing suspicion.

In the meantime, he had to devise a way to give this single scroll back to Major Ying and make it look like the boy snake had been in possession of it.

Ying and his ridiculous carved face, constantly shouting orders and making demands, Tonglong thought. Ying's most recent demand had been that Tonglong return to Cangzhen as soon as his mission of following the boys was complete.

As far as Tonglong was concerned, this mission was accomplished. He climbed down from the tree.

Just one more thing to do, Tonglong thought. Before heading to Cangzhen, he needed to see a man about a boat. Actually, a fleet of boats. It was time he collected some favors. If everything worked out, he would not only be able to give Ying the young warrior monks, he would also give Ying his very own stronghold. Ying would be a very happy young man.

Tonglong, however, would be even happier.

"MALAO!" Seh shouted.

Fu roared and jumped to his feet. He began clawing at the massive stronghold gate. Tree bark flew in every direction.

From behind the gate, Seh heard Malao squeal, and somebody growled, deep and powerful, "Why, you little—"

Seh recognized that voice. It belonged to the bear-style kung fu master, Hung, Mong's right-hand man.

"Open up, Hung!" Seh shouted. He banged on the gate.

"Seh, is that you?" asked another voice from inside the stronghold. Seh recognized that voice, too. It was NgGung.

"Yes!" Seh said. "Open the gate, NgGung! And tell that hairy beast to leave my little brother alone. Malao hasn't done anything wrong."

"Malao is fine," NgGung replied. "Just a moment."

The gate swung open, and Seh slipped inside. The pit of his stomach began to tingle, and the snake gripped his arm tight. Seh ducked.

The back of NgGung's fist spun over Seh's head. "Nice move!" NgGung said. "Welcome to the stronghold!"

Seh's eyes widened. "You're crazy!"

"Thank you," NgGung replied. He turned toward the gate opening and began to spin.

"Be careful, Fu!" Seh shouted. *"Crouching Tiger Comes Out of the Cave!"* Seh glanced over his shoulder and saw Hung leaning against the trunk of a large tree, grinning. Hung's beady black eyes shone bright beneath his massive, hairy brow. Hung folded his arms and rested them on his enormous, jiggling belly.

Fu lumbered through the gate hunched over, like a tiger crouching. NgGung's spinning back fist breezed over Fu's head, and Seh saw one of NgGung's legs begin to rise. Fu must have seen it, too. Fu lifted one knee high to block the kick and thrust two tiger-claw fists straight out with a mighty roar.

Fu's fists connected solidly with NgGung's midsection and NgGung was lifted off the ground. Fu clamped onto NgGung's tattered vest with both hands and dropped to his knees, twisting his body powerfully to one side. NgGung slammed to the ground and Fu jumped on top of him.

NgGung lay in a heap beneath Fu, laughing. "That was fantastic!" NgGung said. "Oh, my back is killing me! Where did you learn that?"

"It's an original," Fu growled. "Where's my little brother?"

"Up here, Fu!" Malao said. "Nice move!"

Seh looked high in the tree Hung was leaning against. Malao was dangling from a thin limb close to the very top.

Hung ran one hand through the greasy mass of thick hair on top of his head and growled at Fu. "You are Sanfu's boy, aren't you?"

"Who?" Fu asked.

"Mountain Tiger," NgGung answered. "That's how we know him. You might know him as the Drunkard."

Fu slammed his fist into the dirt next to NgGung's head. "What do you know about the Drunkard?"

Hung chuckled, low and deep. "He's Sanfu's boy, all right."

"Fu," Seh said, "you can question NgGung later. We need some other answers first." He looked at NgGung, then at Hung. "Why did you attack us?"

Hung scratched his heavy beard. "It's a rite of passage. You should feel honored."

NgGung laughed. "Right! And Hung is still upset that Malao got the best of him! I'd wager he also hasn't forgotten that you were the one who threw Malao the spear, Seh. Hung is still walking with a bit of a limp."

Hung growled.

Seh ignored him. "Where is Mong?"

Hung flashed a sarcastic grin. "He left last night to get AnGangseh. You know who *she* is, don't you?"

"Yes, I know who she is," Seh snapped. "When will they return?"

"Two weeks," Hung said.

"Two weeks!" Seh said. "We can't wait that long. We have to do something now!"

"Don't worry," Hung replied. "We have plenty for you to do now."

Fu rolled off NgGung and stood. "Like what?" he asked.

"Yeah, like what?" Malao said as he climbed down the tree.

NgGung stood and stroked his long, thin mustache. "Well, for one, we have to prepare for the banquet."

Fu's eyes widened. "Banquet?"

"Yes," NgGung said. "The biggest this stronghold has ever seen. But first we need to finish building the banquet hall."

Seh looked at NgGung. "Tell me more."

"Mong has always wanted a banquet hall," NgGung said. "This year, he finally decided to build one. We weren't supposed to finish it until this summer, but when he learned you might be coming here, he ordered us to speed up construction. He told us if you showed up while he was gone to have a banquet ready when he arrives. It will be especially important for him because AnGangseh will be here, too."

Hung nodded. "And since we have to speed things up because of you, you and your brothers are going to help." He pointed to Fu. "You're coming with me, big boy, and your brothers will go with NgGung. We have a lot of work to do. Let's move."

The stronghold was alive with activity. There were many more people inside the stronghold than Seh had imagined. He counted close to two hundred men and women in all.

Seh realized the stronghold functioned like a small town. He saw several blacksmiths and two shops selling food. There were people making clothes and others making shoes and boots. He even saw several buildings overflowing with pigs, chickens, and other animals.

They passed through the buildings and stopped at the edge of an open plateau. It was large, with small pockets of evergreen trees spread in every direction. Seh felt like he was on top of the world.

"It's nice up here, isn't it?" NgGung said.

Seh nodded. "What's that?" He pointed to the skeleton of a very large building.

"That, my friend, is the banquet hall," NgGung replied.

"We have two weeks to finish it?" Seh asked.

"I'm afraid so," NgGung said.

Seh spent what was left of the day in the rafters with NgGung. Malao did, too, but they had very different jobs. Malao leaped from rafter to rafter and scurried up and down support posts getting tools for people, while Seh made his way slowly along each rafter with NgGung, joining the rafters to their supporting beams. Occasionally, Seh caught a glimpse of Fu, dragging enormous sections of lumber to the work site with Hung. Fu did not look happy.

Before leaving the work site for the evening, Seh released the snake for the night like he always did and turned his attention to the three dragon scrolls he had been carrying. He had spread them out to dry on a huge rock earlier, where he could keep an eye on them. They were now ready to be rolled back up.

Seh saw that two of the scrolls contained detailed descriptions of dragon-style kung fu techniques, and one was a basic pressure point chart. On the opposite side of the pressure point chart was a drawing of *chi* meridians—the channels through which energy travels throughout a person's body.

Seh thought the two-sided scroll with the drawings was rather odd. The information in both drawings was knowledge handed down to every kung fu student, regardless of the style they studied. Seh decided that *chi* meridians and pressure points must be especially important to dragon-style kung fu masters.

As Seh began to roll up the scrolls, NgGung approached him.

"I have some information for you," NgGung said.

Seh frowned. "Am I going to have to fight you for it?"

NgGung chuckled. "No, no. This concerns your sister. It's free."

Seh's eyebrows rose.

"There is a price on her head," NgGung said. "My sources seem to think she survived the assault, and the soldiers who attacked Shaolin have been spreading a rumor that Hok assisted them in destroying Shaolin."

"That's impossible!" Seh said.

"I'd agree with you," NgGung said. "However, the damage is done. The soldiers claim that Hok arrived at Shaolin ahead of the troops and opened the gates for them in the middle of the night. They say if it wasn't for her, they never would have gotten access."

"What else do you know?"

"Nothing," NgGung replied. "I'm sorry, Seh."

"We have to do something," Seh said.

"You're right," NgGung said. "And we will, after Mong returns. We can't have the locals believing a former Cangzhen monk was responsible for the destruction of the mighty Shaolin Temple."

Seh looked at NgGung. "Why did you leave Cangzhen?"

"Me?" NgGung said. "Basically, I didn't see eye to eye with Grandmaster. The same is true for the others."

Seh rubbed his long chin. "So you, Mong, Hung, Gao, and Sanfu left Cangzhen and formed a . . . gang?"

"A few others left, too," NgGung said. "Some of them still work with us. Some of them don't."

"And you . . . steal things?"

NgGung frowned. "We don't steal anything. We're

bandits, not thieves. Thieves steal from innocent people for selfish reasons. Bandits intercept shipments of
gold and such from tax collectors."

"How is that not stealing?" Seh asked.

"Because we give it all back to the people,"
NgGung replied.

"Oh," Seh said. "So you don't keep any of the
money?"

"No. Several of the bandits would love to keep at
least a small percentage, but Mong won't allow it.
That's why our stronghold is so independent. Everyone here has a job in addition to being a bandit. We're
very busy."

Seh pointed to the skeleton of lumber that was to
become the bandit banquet hall. "'Busy' is an under-
statement. You really plan to finish that in two
weeks?"

"That's right," NgGung said. "Two weeks."

CHAPTER
13

For two weeks, Seh, Malao, and Fu worked their fingers to the bone. So did the rest of the stronghold's residents. Their efforts paid off. They finished the banquet hall the morning Mong returned.

Seh didn't get to see Mong, but he did get the rest of the day off. He spent his time meditating. Alone except for the snake sleeping coiled on his arm, Seh slipped into a deep trance. He didn't come out of it until early evening. The banquet was in full swing by the time he stepped through the banquet hall's front doors.

The single, gigantic room was illuminated by rows of lanterns that Seh had helped install. He grinned. They looked good. Another project he had helped with was the huge banquet table and long wooden benches. They were filled with more than a hundred bandits clanging bowls and toasting one another. Their laughter echoed around the immense wooden interior.

Spread across the tabletop lay more food than Seh had seen at any ten Cangzhen banquets. There were rice dishes, noodle dishes, soups, buns, vegetables, sweets, meats, fish, nuts—even a few fruits. Seh also saw what appeared to be the leg of a lamb and several baby pigs roasted whole. Thankfully, he didn't see any monkeys, a meat he remembered Hung favored.

"Hey, Seh!" Malao shouted. "Come sit by me!"

Seh glanced at the head of the table and saw Malao sitting near Mong. Gao sat on one side of Malao, NgGung on the other. Malao was wearing a new purple robe and matching pants. Seh wondered where he'd gotten them. Seh was still wearing the same blue silk robe and pants NgGung had given him the night Cangzhen was destroyed.

Malao wasn't the only one to receive new clothes. Fu sat across from Malao, wearing an oversized robe and matching pants made of brilliant white silk. He looked like a big puffy cloud. Hung sat next to Fu.

Seh stifled a grin and headed toward Malao. NgGung and Gao scooted over so that Seh could sit with them. Seh adjusted the three scrolls in the folds of his robe, pulled his sleeve down over the snake on his wrist, and sat down.

Someone growled across the table and Seh glanced over, expecting to hear a complaint about bringing a snake to the dinner table. Instead, he saw Fu and Hung both grabbing hold of the same steamed chicken. Fu had one leg. Hung had the other.

Fu snarled and yanked the chicken in his direction. Hung held fast. Fu was left holding only one leg.

Fu reached for the rest of the chicken, and Hung snatched it away. Hung raised the entire carcass to his face and sank his teeth deep into the breast meat. Golden juice dribbled through his heavy beard down his neck.

Fu's eyes narrowed. He grabbed hold of a whole roast duck and began to lift it to his mouth. Hung dropped the chicken and swiped at Fu's duck with a massive bear-claw fist. Hung connected, his dirty fingernails digging into Fu's duck.

Fu grimaced and let go, slamming his fists on the tabletop. He glared at Hung as Hung tore into the duck.

"Relax, Fu," Seh said. "There's plenty of food to go around. No need to get into a food fight."

"Food fight?" Fu growled. "That's not a food fight. *This* is a food fight!" Fu scooped up a double handful of boiled pig intestines and hurled them at Hung's head.

"ARRRRRRR!" Hung roared. He stood, flinging intestines out of his eyes. Hung picked up a whole smoked cow tongue and raised it high over his head. The long, thick tongue flopped back and forth, painting everyone in the immediate vicinity with specks of brown sauce.

"Hung!" Mong shouted. "Put the tongue down."

Hung's beady eyes narrowed.

"Drop it," Mong said. "Now."

Hung dropped the tongue. It splashed into a large pot of corn chowder.

"Find someplace else to sit," Mong said. "That's an order."

Hung growled and walked to the opposite end of the table.

Malao jabbed Seh in the ribs and began to giggle uncontrollably. "Did you see that? Fu almost got a licking from Hung!"

The bandits burst into laughter. Even Fu grinned.

Seh shook his head and reached for a bowl of pickled carrots. The pit of his stomach began to tingle, and the snake tightened on his arm.

Seh froze. The *chi* energy patterns radiating from whoever just entered the doorway seemed oddly familiar. He spun around on the bench and saw a small, hooded figure slip into the room, clad head to toe in several layers of black silk. An eerie wave of silence washed over the room as the figure glided across the floor in a series of subtle curves, never moving in a straight line. Even Malao quieted down.

Seh heard Gao whisper to Malao, "Whatever you do, don't look into her eyes."

Seh swallowed hard when the woman stopped in front of him. Two small hands emerged from within oversized robe sleeves and slowly lifted back the black hood. What was revealed was the most striking face Seh had ever seen.

The woman's skin was dark, yet seemed to glow in the light of the hall's lanterns. She had full red lips, a tiny nose, and high cheekbones that sloped down to a delicate, angular jaw. And then there was her hair. Luxurious and black as midnight, it cascaded over her shoulders and disappeared beneath her robe, shimmering like a rushing river in the moonlight.

But her most striking feature was her eyes. Long, narrow, and piercing, they were the kind of eyes you would never forget. Ever.

Something stirred deep inside Seh. A memory. There was something incredibly familiar about her eyes—

"I am AnGangseh," the woman said to Seh. "Welcome home, ssson."

..
CHAPTER 14

Seh sat at the banquet table, mesmerized.

"Come with me," AnGangseh whispered, and Seh obeyed. He couldn't help himself. It was as if his legs stood by themselves and carried the rest of him out the back door.

In a daze, Seh followed AnGangseh. Neither spoke until they were alone in a storage shed behind the banquet hall.

AnGangseh set down the small lantern she carried and closed the door behind them. She stared deep into Seh's eyes.

"I'm sssorry we have to meet this way," AnGangseh said in a low, silky voice. "I've missed you."

Seh didn't know what to say. He wasn't even sure

if he could speak. He could hardly see his mother's face in the dim light, but he was transfixed. He knew that *AnGangseh* meant "cobra" in Cantonese and that certain cobras could hypnotize their prey. He thought maybe he should look away—just in case—but he was certain what he was experiencing was far more than some type of trick. Deep down inside, he remembered those eyes.

Seh stared at AnGangseh for a very long time. He couldn't explain it, but the longer he looked at her, the stronger the connection he felt with her. He had never experienced anything like this before.

"You have very ssstrong *chi*," AnGangseh said. "That makes me happy."

Seh nodded.

"Why is it you do not ssspeak?" AnGangseh said. "Are you afraid of me? Embarrassed? Ashamed?"

Seh blinked several times and closed his eyes. His head seemed to clear. "No, I'm none of those. Why would I be?"

"I don't know," AnGangseh replied. "I sssuppose you may have felt abandoned by me and your father."

"No," Seh said, his eyes still closed. "I, uh, never really thought about my past much until Cangzhen was destroyed."

"I want you to know, you pass through my mind every sssingle day," AnGangseh said. "I only wanted a better life for you than Mong and I could provide."

"I understand," Seh said.

"Do you?" AnGangseh asked. "Do you know what

it's like to hand your child over to a complete ssstranger? A ssstranger ssso cold, he gave you the name Sssnake?"

Seh stiffened and opened his eyes. He was drawn into his mother's eyes once more. "You mean my name wasn't always Seh?"

"Of course not," AnGangseh replied. "Just like your brother Fu wasn't originally named Tiger and your brother Malao wasn't originally named Monkey. Grandmaster changed your names to better erase your pasts. He sssaid if he were to raise you, he wanted to ssstart with a clean ssslate."

Seh shivered. "What was my name before Cangzhen?"

"Choy," AnGangseh replied.

"Really?" Seh said. "'Wealthy'?"

"Yes. I wanted you to grow up and amass a fortune ssso that you would not have to live as I have lived with Mong. I wanted you to live as I once lived, long ago."

Seh's mind began to race. "*Choy* is a Cantonese word, and so is *AnGangseh*. Were you a Cangzhen warrior nun?"

AnGangseh laughed. "Me? Never."

"Oh," Seh said. "You really are from Canton, then?"

"Yes."

"So, I am Cantonese?" Seh asked.

"You are half Cantonese," AnGangseh said. "Mong is from the north. Destiny brought me and Mong here."

Seh thought about destiny. His destiny and the

destiny of others close to him. For some reason, the image of Tonglong popped into his mind. Tonglong had felt somehow familiar to him. Seh's head began to spin, but he forced himself to speak. "Do I have any brothers or sisters?"

"You mean, did Mong and I have any other children?"

"Yes," Seh said.

AnGangseh gazed at Seh and smiled. "No."

Seh felt his knees grow weak. "Did you ever—"

AnGangseh's body suddenly went rigid. "Shhh! Sssomething is wrong."

Seh blinked several times, and the pit of his stomach began to tingle. He realized the snake on his arm was shivering.

The shed door burst open.

"On your knees!" shouted an armor-clad soldier. He pointed a *qiang* back and forth between Seh and AnGangseh. They were under attack!

"Do as the man sssays, ssson," AnGangseh said softly. "We don't want to anger him."

Seh dropped to his knees and watched AnGangseh do the same. AnGangseh tilted her head into the lantern's glow and stared up at the soldier.

"Well, hello, beautiful," the soldier said.

AnGangseh batted her eyes at the man.

"Stand and come closer," the soldier said. "I want to get a better look at you."

AnGangseh stood and slithered toward the soldier, raising the hood of her black robe.

"You may just be the most beautiful creature I

have ever laid eyes on," the soldier said. "How about a little kiss?" He puckered his lips.

To Seh's surprise, AnGangseh puckered her lips and leaned toward the soldier.

The soldier smiled and leaned forward.

AnGangseh's full lips parted ever so slightly, and Seh saw a thin line of spit shoot straight into the soldier's eyes. As the man brought his hands up to his face, AnGangseh lunged toward him and sank a vicious snake-fang fist into the man's jugular vein. Seh watched the long nails on her index and middle fingers disappear into the soldier's flesh.

The soldier gasped and stumbled backward, and Seh saw the man's neck instantly swell to twice its normal size. AnGangseh must have poison under her fingernails!

AnGangseh turned to Seh. "Give me the ssscrolls, ssson."

Seh shook his head in an effort to clear it. He wasn't sure he had just heard things right.

AnGangseh knelt in front of Seh and looked deep into his eyes. "I don't have time to explain. We are under attack. If it is Ying, he will be looking for you, your brothers, and the ssscrolls. The workman told me about the dragon ssscrolls you let dry in the sssun. Let me hide them for you. If they are with me, at least I'll have an excuse to sssee you again. You must go to Malao and Fu."

As if in a dream, Seh felt his arm begin to move. His hand reached into the folds of his robe and removed one of the three scrolls he carried. As AnGangseh snatched it from him, her hand brushed against his. It was ice cold and sticky with blood.

"Good boy," AnGangseh said. "Don't tell anyone I have them. The fewer people that know about this, the better. It will be our little sssecret, okay?"

Seh felt his head nod. He reached into his robe and handed her a second scroll.

AnGangseh grinned.

As Seh reached for the final scroll, a voice caught his attention.

"Well, well, well," a soldier said from the doorway. "What do we have here?"

AnGangseh hissed, and Seh turned toward the soldier. Seh blinked several times and shook his head. He saw a group of soldiers run past.

My brothers, Seh thought. He lunged at the soldier in the doorway, but AnGangseh got there first. The soldier stumbled backward and screamed as AnGangseh's fingernails dug into his temples.

Seh slipped past them and headed for the back door of the banquet hall.

"Wait, ssson!" AnGangseh called out, but Seh didn't bother to turn back. His brothers might need him. As he ran, he slid the last scroll along the small of his back up under his robe, beneath his sash. That was still the most secure place for it if he had to fight.

Seh arrived at the banquet hall's rear door and stopped in his tracks. Something didn't look right. He scanned the area in the dim moonlight and realized what it was. The ground was perfectly smooth. Too smooth. There wasn't a single footprint in the sandy soil.

Someone must have recently passed over it using the Invisible Step technique. With every step forward, the person's back leg sweeps the ground behind him, covering his tracks. Seh knew it was very advanced kung fu. He also knew Ying was an expert at it.

Seh slid up to the back door and began to open it slowly.

Seh stuck his head through the banquet hall's back door. Inside, it was pure pandemonium. The front door was open at the opposite side of the hall, and both bandits and soldiers were pouring in and out. Inside the hall there must have been about fifty bandits and one hundred armored soldiers. Several soldiers had *qiang*s.

Seh felt his head begin to cloud from all the activity. He fought it and moved forward.

The instant Seh stepped through the back door, the wide blade of a soldier's broadsword slashed through the air in search of Seh's forehead. Seh dropped to one knee and rolled, and the blade sank deep into the doorjamb.

Seh jumped to his feet, stumbling on something. He glanced down and saw a large, elaborate silk hat lying in the middle of the floor. Irritated, he kicked it out of the way.

The pale head of a well-groomed man rolled out of the hat, turning end over end across the floor.

"Captain Yue!" Seh's attacker gasped.

The soldier went after the head and Seh backed up against the wall. Seh heard someone retch, followed by Hung's voice sounding wet and sloppy. Seh looked in the corner and saw Hung hunched over. Fu was next to him.

"Do it!" Hung growled. "You need to empty your stomach to fight. Don't make me shove my finger down *your* throat, too." Hung shook a bile-covered finger at Fu. Seh saw bits of food clinging to the back of Hung's hairy hand.

Fu extended his finger.

Seh turned away.

"Seh, over here!" Malao shouted. He was standing on top of the banquet table, kicking plates of food into soldiers' faces. Gao was jumping frantically around on all fours next to him. Gao's tongue was hanging out, and his eyes rolled around crazily.

A soldier climbed onto the far end of the table and ran toward Malao and Gao. Gao responded with an unorthodox maneuver that was half dog roll, half foot sweep. The soldier's legs flew out from under him and he toppled to the floor. *Woof! Woof! Woof!*

Seh heard several small bones crunch behind him,

and another man cried out. Seh looked over at the back door and saw NgGung waddle through it into the banquet hall. NgGung laughed in the face of the soldier who had just punched him in the stomach, then knocked the soldier unconscious with a hammer fist. NgGung turned toward the center of the hall and began to spin, cutting a wide swath through the combatants. Seh followed him with his eyes until NgGung passed a soldier with an extraordinarily long ponytail braid. It was Tonglong.

Tonglong was pitted against several bandits, and he wielded his straight sword with great skill. So much so, three of the bandits facing him ran off.

KA-BOOM! A *qiang* fired near Seh.

Yip! Yip! Yip!

"NOOO!" Malao shouted.

Seh looked back at the table. Blood began to squirt out of a wound in Gao's arm. Malao's upper lip curled back, and he pulled the monkey stick from the folds of his robe.

Seh was about to jump onto the table to help Malao when the pit of his stomach began to tingle. He glanced out of the corner of his eye and saw Tonglong staring straight at him.

Tonglong raised his sword and charged toward Seh.

Seh lowered himself into a horse stance and raised one fist to protect his face. He lowered his other fist in front of his midsection as Tonglong attacked.

Tonglong swung his straight sword at Seh's head

and Seh ducked, only to realize too late that Tonglong's swing was just a ploy. Tonglong already had one of his legs cocked, and he unleashed a mighty kick toward Seh's chest. Seh brought his forearms together in time to block the kick, but the powerful impact sent Seh tumbling backward to the ground. As Seh scrambled to get to his feet, Tonglong jumped on top of him.

Seh grabbed the wrist of Tonglong's sword arm with one hand and used his other hand to lash out at Tonglong's neck with a snake-head fist. Tonglong blocked Seh's strike by raising his shoulder and countered by grabbing the front of Seh's robe with his free hand. Tonglong ripped Seh's robe wide open and, to Seh's amazement, jerked free and jumped off Seh.

Tonglong turned and raced toward the center of the hall as Seh stood with his robe spread wide across his chest. Seh watched Tonglong grab a uniformed man and lead him to the fringe of the fighting. The man turned to face Seh. It was Ying.

Tonglong pointed to Seh's exposed chest and handed Ying what appeared to be one of the dragon scrolls. Seh checked the small of his back. His scroll was still there.

Ying tucked the scroll into his own robe and grinned. He flicked out his forked tongue and shrieked, "BROTHER SEH!"

Ying took three strides sideways up the nearest wall and leaped high in the air, his arms spread wide. As Ying soared over the group, Seh sank into a defensive position with one hand held high, the other low.

Ying landed and snapped his right wrist forward. The sharp, weighted tip of his long chain whip shot straight at Seh's head. Seh leaped backward and crashed into the wall. The chain whip missed him, but Ying had snapped it back and began to swing it over his head in a huge circle.

As Ying began to swing faster and faster, Seh felt the pit of his stomach tingle. He glanced out of the corner of his eye and saw Malao running full speed across the top of the table toward them. Malao's upper lip was curled back.

"No, Malao!" Seh yelled. "Don't—"

But Malao didn't stop. One step from the edge of the table, Malao lunged forward in a powerful front handspring. He flipped through the air as Ying lashed out at Seh with the chain whip. Malao scissor-kicked his legs, attempting to kick the sharp, weighted end of Ying's chain whip before it slammed into Seh's skull.

Malao's timing was off. He screamed as the tip of the whip sliced a deep gash across his inner thigh, then fell silent as he hit the wall and his head slammed against the floor.

Seh hissed and lunged forward with a snake-fang fist, aiming for Ying's left eye. Ying tilted his head and Seh's fingers dug into one of the deep grooves in Ying's face. Seh raked his hand downward and Ying's cheek tore open.

At the same time, Seh struck at Ying's neck with his other hand. Ying dropped his chain whip and latched on to Seh's wrist. Then he grabbed Seh's other wrist and began to pull Seh toward him.

Seh unleashed a powerful front kick. Ying blocked it by raising one knee. Seh kicked again. Ying blocked it again.

Ying pulled Seh closer. He opened his mouth wide and hissed, his sharpened teeth glowing in the light of the banquet hall lamps. Ying lowered his face toward Seh's left hand.

The snake beneath Seh's robe sleeve suddenly shot forward and clamped onto Ying's eyebrow. Ying shrieked and swatted at the snake, releasing Seh's hands—but the snake had already let go of Ying and was retreating beneath Seh's sleeve.

Seh heard Hung roar behind him.

Ying shrieked again and spun sideways, narrowly avoiding one of Hung's enormous war hammers. Ying snatched up his chain whip and launched himself out of Hung's reach, disappearing into the fray.

Seh watched Fu pick up Malao's limp body. Fu's eyes were moist.

"Take Malao out the back," Seh said to Fu. "I'll be right there."

Fu nodded and headed for the door.

"You go, too," a voice said beside Seh. It was Mong.

Hung growled. "Where did all these soldiers come from?"

"The shipyard, I suppose," Mong said.

"HaMo—" Hung said.

"Toad?" Seh asked. "Another Cangzhen monk?"

"Yes," Mong replied. "HaMo was in charge of guarding the shipyard."

"Do you suppose he's . . . dead?" Seh said.

"Not yet," Hung replied. "But he will be if I catch him. We've wondered about his allegiance.

Mong looked at Seh. "Why are you still standing here?"

"I don't have a plan—"

"You want a plan?" Mong said. "These soldiers probably docked on the back of the island and climbed up with ropes. You should head in the opposite direction—through the main gate. Take the stairs down and get the boatman who brought you here to take you across. Do what you can for Malao and meet me in the capital city of Kaifeng on the first day of their Dragon Boat Festival at an inn called the Jade Phoenix. There's your plan. Go!"

"What if the boatman won't take us?" Seh asked.

"Then kill him," Mong said. "Kill him and take the boat."

Seh's eyes widened. "Kill him?"

"Listen to me," Mong hissed. "The boatman is HaMo's friend. If the boatman doesn't help you, that means he may harm you. If he doesn't cooperate or if he seems the least bit suspicious, kill him."

"But—"

"Kill him anyway!" Mong roared as Hung shoved Seh toward the door. "Now go! That's an order!"

CHAPTER
16

Seh stumbled out of the banquet hall into the night. Fallen soldiers and bandits now dotted the grounds of the stronghold. Fu and Malao were not among them.

Seh glanced down and saw a trail of blood glistening in the moonlight. It led to the storage shed. He followed it and burst through the door.

Fu was kneeling over Malao, next to the two soldiers AnGangseh had finished off.

"Help me," Fu said, his voice hoarse. Tears fell from his face like rain.

Seh knelt down and saw that Fu had torn several strips from the bottom of his white silk robe. Seh and Fu bound Malao's leg as best they could.

"Are you okay?" Seh asked Fu.

Fu grunted and wiped his face. "I am going to kill Ying."

"Not right now," Seh said. "We need to get out of here." He checked the scroll tucked away in the small of his back and the snake wrapped around his arm. Both were fine. Seh reached into the folds of Malao's robe and removed the carved monkey stick. "You carry Malao. I'll clear the way."

Fu grunted again and lifted Malao. Seh stood and slipped out the door, the monkey stick in his hand.

As they crossed the compound, Seh kept his senses finely tuned for signs of danger. Soldiers were everywhere, but they posed no threat. They lay broken and bleeding in the middle of the main throughway and alongside burning buildings. Bandits were sprinkled about as well, gaping holes ripped through their bodies.

Seh and Fu found the main gate wide open.

"Look down the stairs with those cat eyes of yours," Seh said. "Do you see anything?"

Fu shifted Malao in his arms and peered into the darkness, down toward the lake. "Nope. Do you sense something?"

"No," Seh replied. "But the beach is a long way down. Somebody might be hiding there."

"There's only one way to find out," Fu said. He began to descend the steep stone stairs.

Seh quickly followed, watching Fu's back.

Seh still felt nothing when they reached the small patch of sand that sloped into the lake. He checked the only patch of reeds in sight and found no one.

"At least the boat is still here," Fu said as he climbed in with Malao. "I wish the boatman was, too."

"No, you don't," Seh said, slipping Malao's monkey stick into the folds of his own robe. "Mong ordered me to . . . Never mind. Let's just go."

"Where are we going?" Fu asked.

"To Kaifeng," Seh said. "We're supposed to meet Mong at an inn called the Jade Phoenix on the first day of their Dragon Boat Festival."

"In a month?" Fu asked.

"Yes," Seh replied. He pushed the boat into the water and climbed aboard, taking hold of the long oar. Seh worked the oar back and forth like he had seen the boatman do. The boat moved forward, but steering proved to be far more difficult than he thought it would. Eventually, he found that if he used smooth, steady strokes that traveled the same distance left to right, the boat moved more or less in a straight line.

Seh scanned the lake for other boats. He saw none. Halfway across the lake, he looked over at Fu. Fu was curled around Malao on the floor of the boat.

"What's wrong?" Seh asked.

"Malao won't stop shaking."

"Oh, no," Seh said.

Fu didn't respond.

Seh choked back the sadness welling up inside him. "Are those bandages working?" he asked.

Fu ran his hand over Malao's leg. "I think so. The blood that soaked through is drying."

"That's good," Seh said. "And as long as he's shaking, he's alive. When we get to the beach, we'll take him into the forest and figure out what to do next."

Fu nodded.

"I wish I could make this thing go faster," Seh said. "Do you see any sign of the twins? I haven't sensed them."

Fu lifted his head and scanned the water. "No."

Seh banged his foot on the bottom of the boat three times.

Nothing.

Frustrated, Seh returned his attention to working the large oar. He remained focused on moving the boat forward as quickly as possible. He didn't look back.

Perhaps Seh should have. He might have noticed the small, hollow reed that surfaced in the boat's wake.

He might have also caught a glimpse of the long, thick ponytail braid drifting next to it.

CHAPTER 17

Ying stood inside the banquet hall, flanked by several of his men. He grinned as he listened to the bandit leader's shouts from outside.

"Evacuate! We are no match for the soldiers' *qiang*s! Abandon the stronghold!"

Commander Woo approached Ying. "What should we do?"

"Leave five good men here in the hall with me," Ying replied. "Lead the rest down to the boats. If the bandits escape with the boats, we will be stranded."

"What if they have other boats hidden somewhere and use those to escape?" Commander Woo asked.

"Then let them go," Ying snapped. "We can't spread ourselves too thin. Our men are no match for the bandits individually."

"Understood," Commander Woo said. "Have you heard about Captain Yue, sir?"

"Unfortunately, yes," Ying growled. "I knew he shouldn't have come along. I understand his head is missing. We need to find it. If one of the bandits delivers that head to the Emperor without me there to explain myself, there could be trouble."

"Right, sir. I'll do my best. What about the young monks?"

Ying adjusted his robe, and the scroll Tonglong had taken from Seh pressed against his chest. "Tonglong is following the boys to determine their next move. We'll catch up with those three troublemakers soon enough." Ying glanced over at the large pool of blood where Malao had lain, and smirked.

"Make that *two* troublemakers."

CHAPTER
18

Seh stood on the moonlit beach, staring at Malao in Fu's arms. Malao's dark-skinned face was unnaturally pale, and his whole body continued to tremble.

"Now what?" Fu asked in a hushed tone.

"First we need to get clear of the soldiers," Seh whispered. "Then we need to see if there's anything we can do for Malao. Follow me."

Seh walked along the shore until he found the trail Gao had followed to get to the beach.

"This way," Seh said. "It's risky following a trail, but it will be easier for you to carry Malao." Seh pulled the monkey stick from the folds of his robe. "You go first. I'll watch your back."

About half a *li* into the forest, the pit of Seh's

stomach began to tingle, and the snake on his wrist tightened its grip. Seh stopped to listen.

"What is it?" Fu whispered.

"I don't know," Seh said. "I think someone is following us."

"What should we do?"

"Keep going," Seh said. "Let me know if you see or hear anything."

Two hours later, they were still walking. Seh had stopped often to scan the area, but each time he failed to identify the source of the *chi* he thought he detected. He was beginning to think stress was getting the best of him. Maybe they weren't being followed after all.

Fu finally stopped. "I need to rest," he panted.

Seh shook his head. "I don't know, Fu. We should probably keep moving."

"Then you'll have to carry Malao. I can't take any more of this."

Seh looked at Malao's tiny, unconscious body in Fu's arms. Malao was shaking from head to toe.

"Is that you shaking or Malao?" Seh asked.

"A little of both," Fu said. "My arms are killing me. Let's stop here for the night."

"Here?" Seh said. "We might get caught."

"We're pretty far from the stronghold," Fu said. "I think we'll be okay."

"I don't know—"

"Those soldiers are not going to come this far looking for us tonight," Fu interrupted with a feisty snarl. "And I really don't think anyone is following us. They would have attacked by now."

"Not necessarily," Seh said.

"How many people do you sense?"

"One," Seh replied.

Fu rolled his eyes. "I could beat *one* person with both hands tied behind my back. That's how angry I am." Fu raised his voice. "Does somebody out there want to cross hands with me? Show your face!"

"Shhh!" Seh said.

But it was too late. High in a nearby tree, leaves rustled.

Fu growled and they both looked up. A large, white one-eyed monkey leaped from its perch into an adjoining tree, then scurried down the trunk. It looked like the same monkey Seh had seen leading the troop that raided the bandits' gold carts.

"Uh-oh," Fu said as the monkey began to approach them.

"What are you worried about?" Seh asked. He breathed a sigh of relief. It was the monkey he'd been sensing all along. "That's Malao's friend. Malao mentioned it back at the stronghold."

"Did Malao tell you what that monkey did to Hung's hand?" Fu said. "I saw the scars during our food fight. I'm not taking any chances." Fu took several steps back.

Seh had forgotten about Hung's hand.

The white monkey looked at Malao in Fu's arms, then at the carved monkey stick Seh carried. It locked eyes with Seh and bared an impressive set of four razor-sharp fangs, each as long as Seh's little finger.

"I'm not going to hurt you," Seh said in a soft voice.

The monkey's upper lip curled back and he looked at the stick again.

"Maybe I should put this down," Seh said. He laid the carved stick on the ground and stepped back.

The white monkey rushed over and picked up the stick, then spun around to face Fu. It bared its teeth again.

"Great," Fu said. "Now it's going to beat me with it. Help me out—I've got my hands full with Malao."

Seh took a step toward Fu, and the white monkey shrieked. It jumped up and down, slamming the stick on the ground each time it landed.

Seh stopped. "I don't think it likes me very much."

"You think?" Fu said, rolling his eyes.

Seh took two steps back, and the white monkey took a step toward Fu. Seh took several more steps back, and the monkey took several more steps toward Fu.

"What are you doing?" Fu said. "Get over here!"

"No, wait," Seh said. "I think it wants to see Malao, but it's wary of me. I'm going to take a few more steps back. If it attacks you, I'll be there before you can scream my name."

"Great," Fu said.

Seh took several more steps back, and the white monkey walked all the way up to Fu, its eyes fixed on

Malao's shaking body. Fu held Malao out in front of him and the white monkey slipped the carved stick into the folds of Malao's robe. Then the monkey lowered its nose to Malao's nose and inhaled deeply. It ran a finger across Malao's shaky forehead and scurried away.

Fu looked at Malao, and Seh thought he saw tears welling up in Fu's eyes again. "Ying is going to pay for this," Fu snarled.

"Let's stop here for the night," Seh said. "I think we could both use some rest. I don't sense anyone now that the monkey is gone. Does Malao still have the pouch with the fire stone and metal strike bar?"

Fu glanced at Malao's sash and nodded.

"Maybe Malao will stop shaking if we can warm him up," Seh said. "Step off the trail and stay with him. I'll go find some firewood and a place to spend the night, then I'll come back for you two."

Fu grunted and carried Malao into the underbrush.

"Don't go too far," Seh said. "You'll want to keep your eyes on the trail while I'm gone, just in case someone comes along. We don't want any surprises."

Fu growled, low and deep. "A visit from Ying tonight would be one of the best surprises of my life."

CHAPTER 19

Tonglong raced through the moonlight atop his pitch-black stallion. His wet silk robe and pants clung to his body, his long, heavy ponytail braid slapping his back in rhythm with the horse's powerful strides. He had to hurry.

Tonglong needed to get to the Emperor's summer palace and back to the bandit stronghold in a reasonable amount of time. He didn't want Ying to get suspicious, especially since he'd already accomplished his objective as far as Ying was concerned—find out where the young monks were headed. They were headed to Kaifeng, and that was all Ying needed to know. For now, at least.

Tonglong gripped the sack in front of him, and a

crooked smile rose to his thin lips. He wondered who would be more surprised in the coming days, the Emperor when he was handed his nephew's head or Ying when he found out who had delivered it—and why.

CHAPTER 20

Seh awoke with a jerk, the pit of his stomach tingling. He hadn't even realized he'd fallen asleep. In the bright morning sunshine, he saw the white monkey sitting in a nearby tree, staring at Malao. Fu lay next to Malao, snoring.

Seh decided he must have fallen asleep soon after building a small fire to warm Malao. That was several hours ago. A pile of coals in front of Fu and Malao was all that was left. Seh scanned the area, trying to pick up signs of Ying or his troops. He sensed nothing.

The monkey climbed down, and Seh saw that it carried four long sticks with numerous round objects skewered along each. They were mushroom caps. The

127

monkey dropped the mushroom skewers next to the campfire remains, then sat down beside Malao.

Seh watched, ready to intervene, as the white monkey gently shook Malao like it was trying to wake him. Malao didn't respond.

Seh glanced at the ground around Malao's injured leg. It was dry. At least Malao was no longer bleeding.

The white monkey reached out and began to rub the back of Malao's head. It appeared as though the monkey was mimicking a pressure point massage used to revive an unconscious person. It was the same technique Gao had used to revive the bandit swordsman outside the stronghold.

I wonder where it learned that, Seh thought. *I should have thought to try it.* He sat up, and the white monkey lifted its paw off Malao's short black hair. The monkey bared its teeth. Seh noticed it was staring at his left wrist.

Seh looked down and saw the beauty snake's head poking out of his sleeve. He covered it. He wasn't sure if the monkey was having trouble with him or the snake. Either way, Seh didn't want to take any chances.

"Hey, Fu," Seh said. "Wake up."

Fu didn't flinch.

Seh glanced around and saw a fist-sized rock behind him. He grabbed it and lobbed it at Fu. It bounced off Fu's sizable stomach.

Fu groaned and scratched his belly.

"Wake up, Pussycat," Seh said.

Fu sniffed the air, and his eyes snapped open. He sat up and turned toward the white monkey. The white monkey stared at Fu but showed no signs of aggression.

Fu waved one hand in front of his nose. "That monkey needs a bath more than Malao does. When did it show up?"

"Just now," Seh said. He pointed to the mushrooms. "It brought those, then tried to wake up Malao. It looked like it was trying to massage the base of Malao's skull."

"Good idea," Fu said. "Did it work?"

"It's a monkey, Fu," Seh replied. "Of course it didn't work. I want to try, but I don't think the monkey will let me get near Malao. You're going to have to do it."

Fu looked at the large, one-eyed monkey and hesitated, then grunted and leaned over Malao. The white monkey watched intently but didn't interfere as Fu cradled Malao's head in his hands and began to massage the pressure point.

"Mmmpf," Malao mumbled.

"Hey!" Fu said. "It's working!" He continued rubbing Malao's head, but nothing more happened.

"That's enough," Seh said finally. "We need to find someone who can help keep him awake."

Fu laid Malao's head down. "I wish Hok was here. He . . . I mean, *she* would know what to do."

Seh nodded. "She does know a lot more about these things than we do." He rubbed his long chin. "Too bad we can't go back to the stronghold. I have a feeling AnGangseh might be able to help."

"You mean your mother?" Fu said.

Seh blinked. That sounded strange for some reason. "Yes," he said.

"Why do you think she could help?" Fu asked.

"When the soldiers attacked, she fought off a couple of them with poison hidden under her fingernails. Usually people who handle poisons know antidotes and potions for many things."

"You mean those two dead soldiers in the bandits' shed—" Fu said. "*She* killed them?"

Seh nodded.

"Whoa. What did she want with you?"

"She just wanted to talk."

"Why would she have poison under her nails if she just wanted to talk?" Fu asked.

Seh paused. That was a good question. "I guess because she lives with bandits. She has to be ready for anything."

Fu seemed satisfied with this answer. He nodded and looked at Seh's lower back. "Is that lump under your robe the dragon scrolls?"

"One of them," Seh said. "I gave two to AnGangseh—I mean, my mother—for safekeeping."

"You did *what*?" Fu said. "I risked my life to get those scrolls! When are we going to get them back?"

"The next time we see her, I suppose," Seh said.

Fu growled and slammed a fist into his open palm. The monkey looked at Fu and bared its teeth.

"Take it easy, Fu," Seh said. "You're upsetting the monkey."

Fu snorted and turned away.

"I'm sorry you're angry," Seh said. "But there's nothing we can do about it now. Our number one priority is to get Malao some help. That's what we need to focus on. We need to figure out where to take him."

Fu glared at Seh. "We? How am I supposed to help with that? You led us here. I don't have any idea where we are. What we need is a—" Fu stopped and looked at the white monkey. He slapped his forehead. "A tour guide! Of course!"

"What are you talking about?" Seh asked.

"The white monkey was like a tour guide for me and Malao," Fu said. "It led us to Shaolin Temple. It also led us to the village where the Governor lives."

"How far was the village from Cangzhen?" Seh asked.

"About half a day's travel."

"Was it east of Cangzhen or west?"

"Sort of southwest," Fu said. "Why?"

Seh pointed east toward a small mountain. "The more I look at that, the more I think it's ShiShan Mountain. If I'm right, Cangzhen is on the other side. That means if the village was half a day southwest of Cangzhen, it's probably half a day southeast of where we are now. Do you think the monkey could lead us there?"

"Let's find out," Fu said. He looked the white monkey in the eye. "Can you take us to the village?"

The white monkey tilted its head to one side inquisitively.

"What's the name of the village?" Seh asked.

"I don't know," Fu confessed. He scratched behind one ear and looked at the white monkey again. "Can you take us to the . . . ummm . . . Governor?"

The white monkey seemed to grin. It reached out and grabbed Fu's hand. Seh saw it squeeze three times before letting go and leaping into the trees.

CHAPTER 21

Late that evening, Seh couldn't stop thinking about the mushroom skewers the monkey had brought them earlier. He wished they'd eaten them. He and Fu had been following the white monkey through the forest all day, and he was famished. He was also exhausted. Seh and Fu had taken turns carrying Malao, and it had worn them both out.

Oddly enough, Fu's mind still seemed sharp. He was rambling nonstop about his adventures with Malao. Seh was glad to get the information, but he was finding it harder and harder to absorb the details.

Seh realized he was beginning to feel the effects of too much activity and not enough sleep. His head felt cloudy, and he found it difficult to concentrate. His senses were dull, and he felt increasingly out of touch with the world around him. He longed for something to help him snap out of it.

He soon got his wish.

Fu stopped and shifted Malao in his arms. He raised his nose to the air and inhaled deeply, then smiled. "We're almost there. Come on!"

Fu picked up his pace, and Seh followed. Seh rounded a bend, and a rotten stench hit his nose like a hammer fist. He choked. "What is that smell?"

"The village garbage dump!" Fu said excitedly over his shoulder.

Seh looked into the trees and noticed the white monkey had stopped. "Hey, Fu. It doesn't look like the monkey wants to go any farther."

"That's fine," Fu replied. "I know the way."

Seh nodded goodbye to the monkey, followed Fu around another bend, and came face to face with the biggest pile of trash he could ever have imagined. It was as big around as Cangzhen's largest building and nearly as tall. Tendrils of rank steam drifted skyward in the evening light. He felt nauseous.

"This way," Fu said. He skirted the pile and headed down a narrow trail. The stench of the dump was soon behind them, and Seh's head began to clear.

In no time, they came upon a tall hedge. Fu repositioned Malao and stepped through a section of the hedge that had been trampled to the ground. Seh followed Fu through the gap, and they both stopped in their tracks. Images of the destruction at Cangzhen and Shaolin flooded Seh's mind. The village had been ravaged.

They were standing in the village square, which Seh could tell had once been almost completely surrounded by the tall hedge. The far side of the hedge had been reduced to ash, and Seh had a clear view of the damage beyond. Roofless stone houses and storefronts stood soot-stained and crumbling. Doors and shutters had been burned from their hinges. Not a single building had been left intact.

The pit of Seh's stomach began to tingle as he noticed a group of men step around from behind a structure that stood alone at the head of the courtyard. A blackened sign leaning against the building read Bun Vendor.

The largest of the men froze and stared at Fu. The big man had long, matted hair that was tangled in a scraggly beard. One of his calves was heavily bandaged, as was one of his forearms. He also had bandages wrapped around both thighs. He limped toward them.

"I'll be right back," Fu said. He handed Malao to Seh, and the snake on Seh's wrist slithered up his arm.

Seh laid Malao on the ground as Fu ran toward the large man. Seh focused on the man and noticed the *chi* he emitted was very similar to Fu's. Seh realized that it must be Fu's father, Sanfu.

Sanfu patted Fu roughly on the back, and Fu returned the greeting. Both were grinning from ear to ear. The two of them continued toward Seh and Malao, and their smiles quickly faded.

"Hello, Seh," Sanfu said in a deep, gravelly voice. "It's nice to finally meet you. I wish it were on better terms."

Seh nodded. "Nice to meet you, too, sir."

"No need for formalities," Sanfu said. "I was once a Cangzhen monk, you know. We are brothers." He folded his hands like a Cangzhen monk and looked down at Malao. "What happened?"

"Seh took us to a bandit stronghold, and Ying attacked it," Fu said. "Ying cut Malao with his chainwhip."

"I see," Sanfu said. "Did Ying capture the stronghold?"

"It's possible," Seh said. "His men seemed to have the upper hand. They brought *qiang*s. Many bandits were killed."

Sanfu nodded. "Ying is responsible for the destruction here, too. Amazingly, only a few people were hurt." He looked at Fu. "After Fu and Malao escaped, I stunned Ying with a tiger-claw fist to the head. The villagers and I scattered and hid in the forest. Fortunately, Ying didn't bother to have his men chase us down. But as you can see, he did torch the village."

Seh pointed to the group of men still standing near the bun vendor's shop. "Is that *everyone*? I don't sense anyone else around."

"The women and children have left," Sanfu said. "They went to stay in other places, but some will likely come back after their homes have been made livable again."

"What about the Governor?" Fu asked.

"He has gone to Kaifeng," Sanfu said. "Alone. His son, Ho, is with your friend Ma. Ma's mother took both of them to her sister's house in a neighboring village. I have been staying at her home here, doing what I can to repair it. You boys may stay there with me."

"I'll help you fix it up," Fu said. "I learned a few things about construction at the bandit stronghold."

"Me too," Seh said.

"Thank you," Sanfu said. He looked at Malao again. "Speaking of help, let's see if I can do anything for poor Malao."

Sanfu untied one of several small pouches from his sash and waved the pouch beneath Malao's nose. Malao twitched, and his eyes flew open. He began to mumble incoherently.

"Excellent," Sanfu said. "Malao's sleep is not so deep that we cannot reach him." Sanfu untied a second pouch and withdrew a small decanter. He pulled the plug and dribbled some liquid into Malao's open, babbling mouth.

Malao choked twice and his parched lips closed, followed by his eyes. He stopped mumbling and drifted into unconsciousness.

"I suspect Malao is going to be just fine," Sanfu said.

"What was that drink?" Seh asked.

"Blood tonic," Sanfu replied. "I made a batch for myself after my leg was punctured by a *qiang* ball weeks ago. It's a combination of herbs boiled in water that helps revitalize your blood. It also helps fight off dehydration." Sanfu pointed to Malao's dry lips. "He would not have survived much longer without fluid. You boys should be proud of yourselves for getting him here before it was too late."

"*Proud?*" Fu growled. "I'm *angry*. I am going to get Ying for this and everything else he's done!"

Sanfu sighed. "Ying is very powerful, Fu."

"Then we'll get help," Seh said. "I think Mong will help us." He lowered his head. "If he survived the attack."

"Mong will be fine," Sanfu said. He rested a huge hand on Seh's shoulder. "Did Mong happen to give you any emergency rendezvous plans?"

Seh nodded. "We're supposed to meet him in Kaifeng in a month on the first day of the Dragon Boat Festival."

"Good," Sanfu said. "I'll come with you. Where are you supposed to meet him?"

"An inn called the Jade Phoenix."

"I'm familiar with it," Sanfu said. He looked at Fu. "They make the best soy sauce chicken."

Fu's eyes widened, and he licked his lips.

Seh glanced down at Malao. He thought about how he would hopefully see his father again and how Fu was already with his. Seh looked at Sanfu. "Do you happen to know anything about Malao's father?"

Sanfu paused and scratched his scraggly beard. "I do. This isn't common knowledge, so I'll ask that you keep it among yourselves. Malao's father used to live in this region and was known by most people as the Monkey King. He kept to himself, and very few people ever saw him. He ran off recently. He's not coming back."

"Is he still alive?" Fu asked.

"No one knows," Sanfu replied.

"What was he running from?" Seh asked.

"Not *what*," Sanfu said. "*Who*. Someone called Bing."

"Ice?" Seh said. "That's Cantonese."

"Yes, it is," Sanfu said.

"Then we'll add Bing's name to the list right after Ying's!" Fu said. He slammed his fist into his palm.

Sanfu shook his head. "You are no match for Bing. If you feel you must take action, Fu, focus on Ying. He is too powerful to attack head-on, so you'll have to chip away at him slowly. Start by undoing the evil things he's done.

"I vowed long ago to no longer be part of anyone else's business," Sanfu continued, "but it appears as though I must break that vow. I will help you. We will start with patching up Malao, then we'll do what we can to help the villagers before leaving for Kaifeng and your meeting with Mong. Together, we won't accomplish much, but if you can convince Mong to help us, we might just have a chance."

CHAPTER 22

Two days after he'd captured the stronghold, Ying sat alone at the head of the huge table in the center of the bandits' banquet hall, drafting a report he would submit to the Emperor. Things were going better than he had expected.

Ying had gone into the battle with roughly one hundred soldiers against an estimated one hundred bandits. The bandit body count was seventy. The soldiers, fifty. His men were getting better with the *qiang*s. Next time, he would have his men hunt their enemy down instead of letting them escape.

Ying was about to dip his brush into the bottle of black ink for the finishing touches on his report when someone knocked on the front door. He scowled and set the brush aside. "Enter."

Tonglong walked through the door with one hand behind his back. "Greetings, Major Ying. I have something of great significance for you."

Ying's carved brow rose. "Three young heads with short black hair?"

"No, sir," Tonglong said. "The boys are headed to Kaifeng."

Ying scowled. "All three of them?"

"As far as I know, sir, yes. The small one was unconscious when I last saw him, but he was still alive. The young warrior monks intend to rendezvous with Mong in a month. Assuming Mong is still alive."

"Mong's body is not among the dead," Ying said. "I checked myself." He looked at Tonglong's arm. "What is behind your back?"

Tonglong held out a sheet of fine parchment, rolled up. The paper was of even higher quality than the material Ying was using for his report. Ying noticed immediately that the document carried the Emperor's seal.

"For you," Tonglong said. He bowed.

Ying snatched it out of Tonglong's hand. "Where did you get this?"

"I happened upon the Emperor in the forest and—"

"Again?" Ying interrupted. "You also 'happened upon' the Emperor when I sent you to deliver the Cangzhen Grandmaster's head."

"I know," Tonglong replied, his narrow eyes fixed on Ying's. "I could hardly believe it myself."

Ying could not read Tonglong's expression. "What is this?"

"I don't know, sir," Tonglong said, his eyes still glued to Ying's. "However, if I were to guess, I would say the Emperor wishes to congratulate you on all your recent accomplishments. He already knows about Cangzhen, and I told him about everything that happened here. He seemed most interested in hearing about the events in your words."

Ying fought back a grin and broke the seal on the rolled-up document with one of his long fingernails. It was indeed an invitation. The Emperor wanted to see him in twenty-one days. Something big was being planned. The Emperor rarely invited anyone to his summer palace—Ying had never been there before.

"It looks like I will be busy," Ying said. "You will be, too. Make arrangements for Commander Woo to take a group to Kaifeng to search for the boys. You will stay here and devise a defense strategy for retaining the stronghold in case the bandits return. Train the remaining men in the strategies you feel would be most helpful."

"I have no intention of letting anyone take this fortress," Tonglong said in a matter-of-fact tone. "And I already know how I will lead the men."

"It sounds like you have given this some thought," Ying said as he picked up his brush.

"You have no idea, sir."

"Then get out of my sight and show me what you are made of!" Ying snapped.

"I intend to," Tonglong said with a bow. As he turned and headed for the door, a thin smirk played upon his lips. "I fully intend to."

For three weeks, Seh and Fu put their new construction skills to good use. Seh helped shape and install replacement rafters for numerous roofs while Fu single-handedly cut, stripped, and delivered support timbers to nearly every work site.

When they weren't working, Seh split his time between solitary meditation sessions and trying to cheer up Malao. Malao had regained consciousness after one day in Sanfu's care and he was making a speedy recovery, but he was sad. Sanfu had confirmed that the Monkey King was Malao's father, and Malao now knew that the Monkey King was missing thanks to someone called Bing—or "ice." Malao barely spoke with anyone.

Today, however, things were beginning to turn

around. Malao had gone into the forest early in the morning and found the white monkey. This had made a noticeable difference in Malao's mood. By early afternoon, he was up on the roof of Ma's mother's house with Fu, giggling as he speculated about the size of the hole that would be left in the front yard if Fu happened to slip.

A few houses away, Seh was working with Sanfu. Sanfu was on the ground positioning a new support post while Seh was dangling from a rafter, joining two replacement beams. They were discussing Kaifeng.

"So, we'll leave tomorrow?" Seh asked.

"Yes," Sanfu replied. "First thing in the morning. Malao and I are still moving slowly, so it will take us extra time to get to the section of the road where inns begin to appear. I'd rather not sleep on the side of the road. Too many thieves and other questionable characters lurking about."

"I heard it will take us six or seven days to walk there," Seh said, pulling a large wooden mallet out of his sash.

"That's right," Sanfu said. "Probably seven. That would put us in the city on the fifth day of the fifth moon—day one of Kaifeng's Dragon Boat Festival."

"I'm looking forward to it," Seh said. "I've never been to a big city." He began to pound a long peg, joining the beams to the post that Sanfu was holding.

Sanfu raised his voice. "It certainly is an experience. You've never seen so many people in your life. It's good that you'll have Mong to show you around. He's very familiar with the city."

Seh nodded. "I want to see him again." He paused his pounding mid-swing. He'd had something on his mind for a couple of weeks. "Do you think Mong will bring AnGangseh?"

Sanfu scratched his scraggly beard and looked up at Seh. "I don't know. She is rather . . . independent."

"I noticed that."

Sanfu looked surprised. "So you've met?"

"Yes," Seh said, starting to work again. "Once. She introduced herself at the stronghold."

"That's good," Sanfu said. "Very good."

Seh thought Sanfu sounded sincere. He decided to ask a more personal question. He stopped pounding again. "What do you think of AnGangseh?"

Sanfu's body stiffened and he looked at the ground. "Well, I . . . haven't spent enough time around her to form an opinion. Why do you ask?"

"I don't know," Seh said. "I guess I haven't formed an opinion of her, either, but I entrusted her with two of the dragon scrolls from Cangzhen."

Sanfu stared up at Seh. "You did *what*?"

"I met her just before Ying attacked," Seh said. "She told me to give the scrolls to her for safekeeping, and it sounded like a good idea at the time. Do you think I made a mistake?"

Sanfu shook his head. "I don't know. It seems strange that she would want them. Maybe she was just trying to help. Weren't there four dragon scrolls?"

"Yes," Seh replied. "I still have one scroll. Ying has the other."

"Well, there's not much we can do about it now,"

Sanfu said. "Can I see the one you have? I've seen all the Cangzhen tiger scrolls but never a scroll from another animal style."

"Sure," Seh said. He set the mallet down and reached inside his robe. He pulled out the scroll, careful to keep the beauty snake concealed under his sleeve. Seh dropped the scroll down to Sanfu.

Sanfu opened it. He stared at the *chi* meridian sketch on one side and the pressure point sketch on the other. "This is basic material that all Cangzhen monks learn. Are you sure it's a dragon scroll?"

"I think so," Seh said. "It has dragon characters in several places, and it was among the ones Ying stole."

"I suppose," Sanfu said.

Seh glanced down at the sketches as Sanfu lifted the scroll up to the bright sunlight. "I—" Seh's voice caught in his throat.

"What is it?" Sanfu asked.

Seh stared at the pressure point sketch on the back of the scroll. As Sanfu held the scroll up to the sunlight, the *chi* meridian sketch on the front showed through and the two sketches merged together. The *chi* meridians became roads or rivers, and the pressure points lined up along them like landmarks.

"I don't believe it," Seh said. "It's a map! See how it looks when you hold it up to the sun?"

"Amazing," Sanfu said, tilting his head to one side. "It is indeed a map. Excellent observation."

"Do you recognize anything?" Seh asked.

Sanfu shook his head. "I've crisscrossed this entire region, and I'm certain none of these places are here. Perhaps it's Canton. Grandmaster was from Canton, and he's the one who brought the scrolls to Cangzhen."

"AnGangseh is from Canton," Seh said. "Maybe she'll know."

"It's possible," Sanfu said. "Maybe that's why she wanted them. Maybe we'll get lucky and she'll be in Kaifeng. Now let's hurry and finish up what we can here as soon as possible so that we can get a good night's rest. I want to leave before dawn tomorrow."

Sanfu wasn't kidding about leaving before daybreak. Seh felt bad that Malao had to find the white monkey in the dark to say goodbye. As Sanfu pointed out, they would be traveling on a road frequented by humans, so it was likely Malao wouldn't see his friend for a while.

When Malao had finished his farewell, he followed Seh to the bun vendor's shop to meet Fu and Sanfu. Sanfu gave them each a tattered gray peasant's robe to change into to help them blend in, and the bun vendor loaded up a sack with enough buns for several breakfasts.

"We'll skip lunch while we're traveling," Sanfu explained as he threw the sack over his shoulder, "and eat like the Emperor at supper time."

By the time they thanked the bun vendor and stepped outside, everyone that remained in the village had gathered in the square to see them off. Goodbyes were exchanged, and before the sun had risen, they were on the road to Kaifeng. It was nothing more than a well-worn trail at this point, but Sanfu assured them it would widen twentyfold by the time they reached the gates of the region's capital.

"We should break into two groups," Sanfu said as the sun came up. "Malao, since you and I are both still hobbling about, I suggest you travel with me today." He tossed a small pouch to Fu. "Fu, you and Seh go on ahead. The pouch contains enough coins to get us all a nice meal and lodging for the night. Sometime around sunset, pick a place for us to stay. Feel free to order up some food while you wait for Malao and me."

"I think I can manage that," Fu said with a smile.

Sanfu looked at Seh. "There are some unscrupulous types all along this road, and the innkeepers are no exception. Be careful. If any place seems the least bit suspicious, leave and find another one. It is much better to be safe than sorry—especially out here."

"I understand," Seh said.

Fu didn't seem to be paying the least bit of attention. He licked his lips as if in a dream. "Do you think the inns will serve chicken?"

"For a price, they'll serve you just about anything," Sanfu said.

"What are we waiting for?" Fu said. "Come on, Seh!" He clapped his hands once and raced up the road, reciting a menu fit for the Emperor. "Savory smoked chicken livers, pheasant feet, lark's tongue—"

Seh shook his head and followed, grateful that he didn't hear Fu list Greasy Goose.

149

The road to Kaifeng made for easy travel. Seh didn't have to dodge thorns or tree limbs or sinkholes. He didn't even have to check for landmarks or continuously watch the treetops for the white monkey. All he had to do was follow the road. It was incredibly boring.

After walking the entire day, they had only passed a handful of travelers, all of whom were headed in the opposite direction. None offered a greeting.

The trail they had started out on had grown to an actual road wide enough for four people to walk side by side. Ruts were worn into the center, where carts of various sizes had passed, making for uneven footing. Seh wondered how Sanfu and Malao were managing with their injured legs.

The plan was for Seh and Fu to find a place to eat and rest, but so far, the few ramshackle places they'd had seen had all given Seh a bad feeling. Even the snake on his arm had seemed leery of them, so he hadn't bothered to enter any. Another one was coming into view, and the pit of Seh's stomach began to tingle. Seh shook his head. More bad feelings.

"What about this one?" Fu asked.

"I don't think so," Seh said. He looked at the freshly painted sign, its gold characters shimmering in the late-evening sun. The Divine Dumpling Restaurant & Inn.

"What's wrong this time?" Fu snapped.

"It's a little *too* inviting."

Fu rolled his eyes. "It's getting late, and I'm starving. We're going in." He pushed his way past Seh and barged through the ornate wooden door.

Seh glanced around. Something didn't feel right, but he couldn't put his finger on it. Against his better judgment, he followed Fu inside. The restaurant's interior didn't make him feel any better. It was even more inviting than the exterior. It was small but elegant. Five delicate tables were covered with fine cloth and surrounded by ornate chairs. The dark wood walls and floor were spotless. The entire place felt sterile. There were no customers.

Fu was already sitting at a table, his feet resting on an empty chair. "What do you think? I sure know how to pick them, don't I?"

"I don't like it," Seh replied.

"Whatever," Fu said, glancing at the menu board. "House Special Dumplings. Yummm. I wonder if they'll have meat in them—"

"What kind of question is that?" interrupted a shaky, high-pitched voice. "Of course they have meat! Unlike any you've ever tasted—guaranteed."

A frail old woman stepped out from behind a red curtain at the back of the restaurant and headed for Fu.

"How are they prepared?" Fu asked.

"In a delectable chicken broth," the woman replied.

Fu grinned.

"How much do they cost?" Seh asked.

The old woman stopped next to Fu and bit her lower lip. She glanced at their tattered robes. "Well, normally, we charge an arm and a leg. Our House Special Dumplings really are quite special. We use a secret ingredient that gives them a full-bodied flavor." She poked Fu in the stomach. "However, you, dear boy, look famished, and you appear to be a true lover of food. I'll tell you what—I'll give you a discount. Half price. What do you say?"

"It's a deal!" Fu said.

"Hold on," Seh said. "We don't even know what the full price is. Stop thinking with your stomach."

Fu untied the pouch of coins from his sash and dumped them on the table. "Is this enough?"

The old woman smiled. "More than enough."

"Two more people will be joining us," Seh said. "And we will all need one night's lodging as well."

"We have plenty of space," the old woman replied. "We can talk about the cost of the rooms and meals after your friends arrive. I'm sure I can give them a discount, too. When do you expect them?"

"We're not exactly sure," Fu said.

The woman's thin white eyebrows rose. "Oh? Do they know to meet you here?"

Fu looked at Seh. "I didn't even think of that."

Seh shook his head.

"I'll tell you what," the old woman said. "I'll take a chair and sit out front while you eat. Tell me what they look like and I'll call them over. Okay?"

"Thanks!" Fu said.

The old woman smiled. "I'll get your food first. Two bowls of House Special Dumplings coming right up!"

"Excuse me," Seh said. "If you don't mind, I'd prefer a bowl of vegetable soup or something similar. I don't eat meat."

"Of course," the old woman said. She disappeared behind the curtain.

Fu sat back in his chair and sighed. "Ah, this is the life. I like this place."

"Well, I don't," Seh said. "I sense somebody else in the back." He stood and stepped away from the table.

"Where are you going?" Fu said. "That's probably just the cook."

"Shhh! Keep your voice down. I want to take a look around." Seh was casually stepping toward the red curtain when the old woman burst through it, carrying two large, steaming bowls.

"Going somewhere?" the old woman asked Seh with a smile.

"I was just . . . stretching my legs."

"Please sit down," the old woman said. "Your soup tastes best when it's hot." She looked at Fu. "The same is true for your dumplings, dear. Eat up! I'll be back in a few moments to help find your friends." She disappeared behind the curtain again.

"That was strange," Seh said as he sat down. "The food came so fast."

"You're strange," Fu replied. "Stop analyzing everything and eat." Fu grabbed a pair of chopsticks and a spoon and dove into his dumplings.

"Whoa!" said Fu. "These are the best dumplings I've ever tasted! The broth is really good, too. How's your soup?"

"I haven't even touched my spoon yet," Seh said. He picked it up and began pushing around the pieces of pickled cabbage and leeks inside his bowl. The pit of his stomach tingled.

"You don't know what you're missing," Fu said. "This is absolutely delici—" He stopped in mid-sentence, and his face went sour. Fu fished around inside his mouth with two fingers and pulled out a long black hair. He wiped it on the table and went back to eating.

Seh frowned. "Was that inside a dumpling?"

Fu nodded.

"And you're going to keep eating them?"

"Sure," Fu mumbled between mouthfuls. "It's only a hair."

Seh shook his head and stared at the piece of hair. "Interesting. That hair is long and black, but the innkeeper's hair is gray."

"It probably belongs to that cook you sense," Fu said. "Stop being so—" He set his chopsticks down and gripped the edge of the table with both hands.

"What's wrong?" Seh asked.

"All of a sudden, I feel . . . strange . . . ," Fu said. "I—" Fu's eyes rolled back, and his head slumped forward.

"Fu?" Seh whispered.

Fu was out cold.

I knew something was wrong, Seh thought. *The dumplings were drugged. I'm sure my soup has been drugged, too. What is that woman up to?*

Seh decided to play along. He quickly spooned some of his soup into Fu's bowl so that it would look like he'd eaten some. Then he narrowed his eyes to slits, let his head flop to one side, and slowed his breathing.

A few moments later, Seh saw the old woman appear from behind the curtain with an equally frail old man at her side. The woman held a gigantic cleaver. The old man held a large meat hook in one hand and two coils of rope in the other.

The old man looked at Fu and whistled. "Get a load of that mountain of flesh! The heavens are smiling on us today. He'll stuff enough dumplings to feed an army. Not much meat on the other one, though."

"Free meat is free meat," the old woman said. "I'll

take whatever I can get. You should be able to salvage at least a couple of fillets from the skinny one."

"What about their friends?" the old man asked.

"They said their friends don't even know they're in here. If the others are as scruffy as these two, they'll never think to look inside an establishment as fine as ours. And if they do show up, we'll add them to the menu, too." The old woman cackled. "Let's get to work."

CHAPTER 25

Ying stood before the gates of the Emperor's summer palace, preparing for the accolades that were sure to be the reason behind his special invitation. He had destroyed Cangzhen and taken the bandits' stronghold. It was time to celebrate.

This was, after all, a place for relaxation. Business was for the main palace in the Forbidden City, hundreds of *li* to the north. Ying was ready for a party—in his honor.

Ten thousand things ran through Ying's mind. First and foremost was, *What's taking this fool guard so long to open the gates?*

When the gates eventually opened, Ying rushed in, eager to greet the Emperor. However, after two steps, he stopped, frozen in his tracks. Ying found himself at the far end of what had to be the most magnificent courtyard in all of China.

Thousand-year-old cypress trees stood alongside ankle-high flowers only hours old. Elaborately designed pagodas wrapped themselves seamlessly around natural rock formations that were shaped like Chinese characters. Peacocks roamed freely along the footpaths, and songbirds filled the trees. The centerpiece was a massive man-made lake in the shape of a lotus flower.

Ying had heard rumors that the Emperor had squandered untold fortunes to create this sanctuary for himself and his closest advisors and that it was the most beautiful place beneath the heavens. Until that moment, Ying had dismissed the rumors. However, he now believed every word. He was standing at the edge of it, and *he* had been invited.

Ying closed his eyes and took a deep breath, soaking it all in. Instead of feeling peaceful, though, he sensed someone focusing on him from the lake. Ying opened his eyes and squinted in the bright afternoon sunshine reflecting off the lake's surface. He saw the silhouette of a lean man in an orange robe.

"What are you waiting for?" the man by the lake purred. "I don't have all day."

Ying scowled. It was General Tsung, the leopard-style kung fu master and former Shaolin monk who had successfully destroyed Shaolin Temple—and almost choked Ying to death.

"What are you doing here, Spot?" Ying asked as he walked along the path beside the lake toward Tsung. Tsung's orange monk's robe flapped in the breeze.

"I suggest you reconsider the manner in which you address me," Tsung said. "I outrank you, and we both know I'm the superior fighter. One more comment like that and I'll have your head." He turned and began walking toward an enormous building on the far side of the lake. "Follow me."

Ying bit his lip. There was no point in making a scene in front of the Emperor. At least, Ying assumed the Emperor was nearby. "Where is everyone?" he asked.

"There are soldiers stationed at regular intervals along the compound walls," Tsung replied. "You can't see the men or the walls because the Emperor went to great expense to ensure everything was hidden from view with evergreen foliage."

"I mean, the Emperor and his other guests," Ying said.

Tsung raised one bushy eyebrow. "There is only one guest. A judge. He and the Emperor are waiting inside the palace for you. There is a special chamber designed specifically for situations like yours."

Ying grinned. *A special chamber,* he thought. *And a judge. This must be something significant.*

They reached the palace, and Ying followed Tsung through a maze of elaborately furnished halls. When they reached a door at the end of a long hall, Tsung turned to Ying. "Give me your weapons."

Ying hesitated.

"You will not be allowed inside otherwise." Tsung's jaw muscles rippled.

Ying shook his right wrist, and his chain whip slipped out of a special pocket in his oversized sleeve. He frowned and reluctantly handed it over. The grooves in his face deepened.

"This way," Tsung said, opening the door.

Ying entered and glanced around as Tsung bolted the door behind them. The room was surprisingly large. It was two levels high, the higher one being a balcony. That's where the Emperor stood in his brilliant yellow silk robe and large yellow silk hat. A second man stood on ground level wearing a black robe and small black judge's hat. Around the perimeter of the first floor were close to a hundred soldiers, each armed with a *qiang*.

Tsung clapped once and every soldier pointed his *qiang* at Ying.

Ying stared up at the Emperor, confused.

"What do you have to say for yourself?" the Emperor asked.

Ying tried to make sense of the question and what he saw around him. "Thank you?"

"Thank you!" the Emperor bellowed. He glared down at Ying.

"Thank you, *Your Highness*?" Ying said.

"Do you know why you are here?" the Emperor snapped.

"I believe I do," Ying replied. His eyes darted around the room.

The judge cleared his throat and opened a sizable

scroll. "Major Ying, you are under arrest for negligence in the line of duty."

Ying's eyes widened. "Under arrest? What did I do?"

"You failed to protect my nephew, Yue," the Emperor said. "He was your captain."

"With all due respect, Your Highness," Ying said, "he lost his life while taking the bandit stronghold. He went down fighting—like a soldier. We were victorious."

"Try telling that to my sister," the Emperor said. "I couldn't stand him personally, but my sister seemed rather fond of him."

"I . . . I don't understand," Ying said.

"He was under your command, and he lost his life," the Emperor said. "You are responsible. There is also the matter of your failure at Cangzhen Temple."

"Failure?" Ying said. "I'm sorry five young warrior monks escaped, Your Highness, but other than that, the mission was a success."

"What about the Grandmaster's head?"

Ying twitched. "Didn't my man Tonglong deliver it to you?"

"No," the Emperor replied. "The only head he brought me was Yue's."

Ying scowled and fought the urge to spit on the floor.

"Does that upset you?" the Emperor asked. "Well, how about this—I've rewarded Tonglong by giving him your troops as well as your title. You've officially been stripped of it."

Ying's lips curled back, and his entire body began to shake. He struggled to form words. "When did Tonglong know this?"

"Before he delivered the invitation to you."

Ying snarled. "What is to become of me?"

"You will be punished."

"How?"

"Slowly," the Emperor said. "You will sit in prison until the flesh rots off your bones."

CHAPTER 26

This can't be, Seh thought. *Those dumplings Fu ate . . . ? And that long black hair . . . ?* Seh's stomach began to turn, and he swallowed hard. How many of those dumplings did Fu actually eat?

The only thing that kept Seh from retching was the sound of approaching footsteps. The old man and woman were coming toward him. He closed his eyes completely.

"Hurry up and tie them down," the old woman said. "You know how quickly that sleeping broth wears off."

Seh sensed the old woman walk past and heard her lock the front door. When he sensed the old man hover over him, Seh made his move. He opened his eyes and thrust both arms out, latching on to the man's throat. Seh wasn't about to become somebody's dinner.

The old man dropped the ropes and the meat hook and grabbed hold of Seh's arms, just below the elbows. The old man began to squeeze and Seh cried out. The old man wasn't frail at all. He was incredibly strong, and he was clamping down on pressure points in Seh's forearms.

The old man laughed. "You should never judge a book by its cover, boy." He squeezed harder, and Seh nearly collapsed. Seh struggled to focus enough to lift one knee so he could kick the old man away.

"Eeeeeow!" the old man suddenly shouted, and released Seh. The man took a step sideways and lifted one of his arms. Seh saw blood trickling out of a snakebite.

Seh caught a glimpse of the beauty snake slipping back beneath his robe sleeve. He stepped toward the man but sensed trouble from the rear. Seh ducked just in time. The old woman swung her meat cleaver at his head powerfully from behind. She wasn't the least bit frail, either. Seh realized he was going to have to use every bit of force he could muster.

From his crouched position, Seh slid forward, throwing all his weight into a punch to the side of the old man's left knee.

"Arrrgh!" the old man shouted as he tilted toward the floor. He fumbled for his meat hook. "I'm going to string you up and fillet you into—"

"Quiet, old man!" Seh shouted. He rose and slammed his fist into the old man's jaw, hitting exactly halfway between the man's ear and chin. The old man dropped like a rock, out cold before he hit the floor.

Seh sensed something behind him again and turned to see the old woman launch the meat cleaver at the center of his back. He shifted his weight to one side and watched the cleaver graze his gray cotton robe before it sank deep in the far wall.

The old woman shrieked and headed for the curtain at the back of the restaurant. It took Seh three steps to catch her. A sharp yank on the back of her collar stopped her dead in her tracks, and a single arm around her neck brought her to her knees. Seh hissed in her ear. "If you ever—"

The front door suddenly exploded off its hinges. Sanfu barreled into the room shoulder first. "I heard you shout . . ." He stopped and stared at the old couple. His upper lip curled.

"What are you doing here?" he demanded. "I thought the Governor locked you and this butcher husband of yours away months ago."

Seh released the old woman. She glared at Sanfu. "The *Emperor* recently overturned that decision."

Sanfu scoffed. "So the Emperor has lowered himself to taking bribes from murderers and thieves?"

"I'll be sure to tell him you said that," the old woman spat. "He comes here when he's at his summer palace."

"I'll bet he does," Sanfu said. "Seh, tie her up. Tie up her husband, too. We're spending the night here."

Seh nodded and scanned the room. "Where is Malao?"

"Guarding the back door," Sanfu replied.

"Seh?" a deep, groggy voice said. "What . . . what's going on?"

Seh glanced over and saw Fu rubbing his eyes. "You were drugged, Pussycat," Seh said. "Go back to sleep."

Fu sat up and groaned. "I think I'd rather go back to following the white monkey through the forest. Ohhhhh. How many more nights are we going to have to do this before we get to Kaifeng?"

"Five," Seh replied. "But from now on, I'm picking the inns. And no more dumplings."

CHAPTER 27

"Are you okay, Seh?" Malao asked. "You don't look so good."

"I'll be fine," Seh replied. "Let's just go."

Seh stepped out of their fifth inn in as many nights. He squinted in the early-morning haze and took a long, slow breath. It was the beginning of their fifth day on the road to Kaifeng, and the closer they got to the city, the worse he felt. Even at this hour, hundreds of people flowed along the road before him, like ants hunting for food. His head was beginning to cloud, but he fought it.

Sanfu put a beefy arm around Seh's shoulders. "Only a few more hours to Kaifeng."

Seh nodded and followed as Sanfu pushed his way

into the crowd. Fu and Malao trailed close behind Seh. Seh double-checked the dragon scroll in the small of his back and the snake on his wrist. Both were secure, though the snake was trembling. Its senses were being overloaded, too.

Seh had never experienced anything like this. Since they had left the Divine Dumpling, the road had continued to widen until twenty men could now easily stroll down it side by side. The people traveling along it in both directions carried every object imaginable—live chickens, grain, shoes, tea—the list was endless. Goods were carried on mules, in carts, and on shoulders.

The variety of travelers seemed endless, too. Merchants, craftsmen, and peasants all pushed headlong beside one another, wearing gray threadbare cotton, shimmering silk robes, and everything in between.

It was lunchtime when they reached the massive wooden gates of Kaifeng. The gates were as high as four men were tall and designed to keep intruders out of the walled city. Today they were wide open. A river of more than a thousand people ebbed and flowed in and out of the gates. People pushed up against Seh from every side as they entered the city.

But the worst part was the stench. Between the unending walls of shops along the city's main thoroughfare and the high surrounding walls, there was no air circulation. The combined stink of animal dung, open-air-cooking-stall steam, and human sweat seeped into his nostrils. Seh coughed.

Sanfu muscled his way up to Seh. "It's normally not this crowded," he said. "The first day of New Year and the first day of the Dragon Boat Festival are the worst." Fu and Malao finally pushed through the throng and joined them. "Stay together and follow me," instructed Sanfu.

Sanfu moved forward, parting the crowds, and stopped at the base of an enormous bell tower raising its head high above the masses. Seh was so preoccupied with everything at ground level, he hadn't noticed it until now.

Sanfu pointed at the tower. "Remember this structure. You can see it from anywhere in Kaifeng. Notice it's positioned on the main thoroughfare, which runs south to north. Follow the road south and you'll go

back the way we just came to the primary city gates. Go north and you'll run into a wide bridge that spans the Yellow River. We're now going to head east."

They pushed their way down a side avenue. The farther they went, the fewer people there were milling about. They passed row after row of two-story housing interspersed with small shops offering any item you might need or want. Seh saw grocers, bakers, bankers, and blacksmiths. Like the line of travelers on the road, the list of goods was endless.

After a quarter of an hour, Sanfu stopped in front of one of the small shops. It looked exactly like every other small shop, except it didn't have a sign. Instead, it had a small metal phoenix in the very center of the front door. The phoenix was painted green.

Sanfu knocked on the door three times. A moment later, the phoenix rotated up and Seh saw a big brown eye look out of a hole in the door.

"Sanfu!" a woman said from behind the door. "Come in! Come in!"

The door swung inward, and Sanfu bowed. "Greetings," he said. "It is good to see you." He motioned inside.

Seh entered first. He nodded to the large woman holding the door open and scanned the room. He saw nine or ten small, battered tables, surrounded by mismatched chairs. All the shutters were drawn, and the medium-sized room was lit by too few lanterns. Seh supposed the low light level hid aspects of the place better left in the dark. There wasn't a single customer, and he wasn't surprised.

Fu entered next, followed by Malao. Sanfu entered last, quickly scanning the street before closing the door and locking it.

"Welcome to the Jade Phoenix!" the woman said. "My name is Yuen. You must be Seh, Malao, and Fu. Mong told me you'd be coming."

One corner of Seh's mouth rose in a lopsided grin. Mong was still alive.

"Hello," Seh said.

"Hi," Malao and Fu said in unison.

Sanfu smiled. "So, Mong is here?"

"Yes," Yuen replied. "He survived that terrible attack on his stronghold, thank the heavens. But he's in a meeting right now. He said if you arrived, he

THE
F
I
V
E
A
N
C
E
S
T
O
R
S

170

wanted you to join in—but the boys are to wait here in the dining room."

Seh's grin faded. How did Mong know that Sanfu was with them?

"I understand," Sanfu said. "Is it possible for you to serve these young men some food while they wait? Seh and Malao are vegetarian, but I know Fu would love to sample some of your famous soy sauce chicken."

The woman's eyes lit up. "Certainly! Will you be eating, too?"

"Later," Sanfu said. "After the festivities. Are the dragon boats scheduled to race this afternoon?"

"Yes," the woman replied. "They should start in a few hours."

"Perfect," Sanfu said. He looked at Seh, Malao, and Fu in turn. "Have a seat and relax. This place may not look like much, but the food is outstanding. Trust me." He nodded to the woman, and she blushed. "I will return shortly." Sanfu headed for a long, tattered curtain at the back of the restaurant, and the woman followed.

Seh watched them pass behind the curtain. He wondered why Mong would want to see Sanfu without him or his brothers around.

Fu plopped into the nearest chair. "I don't know about you two, but I'm starving."

"Me too," Malao said.

Seh didn't respond.

Malao looked at Seh. "Are you feeling better?"

"I'm fine," Seh said. "I just have something on my mind." He lowered his voice. "I want to look around. If anyone asks about me, tell them I went to find a toilet."

"Don't tell me you're worried about the filling in their dumplings?" Malao said. He giggled.

Fu rolled his eyes.

Seh remained serious. "Will you cover for me or not?"

"I'll cover for you," Fu said. "But it will cost you half of your lunch."

Malao giggled again.

Seh shook his head. "It's a deal," he said, and headed for the tattered curtain.

CHAPTER 28

Seh found himself in a small kitchen at the back of the Jade Phoenix. He was alone.

Where did Sanfu and Yuen go? Seh wondered. He looked around for a back door. There wasn't one. All he saw was an open window. *They wouldn't have climbed out the window. There must be a trapdoor somewhere.*

Seh scanned the wooden floor. It was pockmarked and stained and warped in several places, but there was no sign of a door anywhere.

Then he looked up.

The ceiling, like the floor, was made of staggered slats of wood. Years of dust and grime had accumulated across the length of the ceiling, but in one corner,

Seh noticed a faint, square-shaped outline where the dust had been disturbed in four perfectly straight lines. The square was just large enough for an adult to pass through.

An attic, Seh thought. *I wonder what's so important that Mong and Sanfu need to hide to discuss it. Hmmm.* Seh glanced at the open, sun-filled window. *Maybe I can just listen in for a moment. . . .*

Seh stuck his head out the window and saw a thick terra-cotta drainpipe running up the side of the building, within reach. He shimmied up it, stopping when he reached a Jade Phoenix medallion like he'd seen on the front door. Only this one was as big as his head.

I wonder . . . , Seh thought as he gently pushed on one side of the green medallion. *Yes!* The medallion pivoted up the slightest amount. Seh pressed his eye to a small opening and was able to see inside a surprisingly large, well-lit room. He could hear clearly, too.

Mong, Sanfu, Hung, Gao, and a well-dressed man Seh didn't recognize sat around a circular table. Yuen bent over and opened the trapdoor, then dropped a rope ladder through the hole. "Ugh!" she said as she began to climb down. "I'm getting too old for this." Her wide hips stuck briefly, but then she was free and clear.

"Thanks for the tea," Sanfu called after her.

"Anytime, dear," she said. "Anytime."

The well-dressed man leaned over and pulled up the ladder, then silently closed the trapdoor. "Where were we?" he asked with an air of authority. "Ah, yes—the new emperor. He is now letting all manner of riffraff into our region. I'm concerned."

"Me too," Sanfu said. "Did you know that Old Man Butcher and his wife are back in business?"

"The cannibals?" Mong asked.

"The very same," Sanfu replied. "Seh and Fu stumbled into their establishment on our way here."

"It's true," the well-dressed man said. "The Emperor reversed my decision to keep them in prison."

Seh's eyes widened. *That man is the Governor!* he thought. *Wait until I tell Fu!*

Sanfu turned to Mong. "Seh took care of both of them single-handedly. It was impressive."

Mong smiled. Seh felt himself smile, too.

"And another thing," Sanfu said. "Seh discovered that the dragon scroll he carries is a map."

Sniff. Sniff. "A map?" Gao said. "Of what?"

"We couldn't tell," Sanfu replied.

Mong rubbed his huge, pale bald head. "Seh arrived at the stronghold with three scrolls. What happened to the other two?"

"Seh gave them to AnGangseh," Sanfu said. "I'm surprised you don't already know this."

"AnGangseh!" Hung growled. "What is she up to now?"

"Hush," Mong said. "She probably took them for safekeeping."

"Safekeeping, my—" Hung began to say.

"That's enough," Mong interrupted. He turned to

Sanfu. "I haven't seen AnGangseh since the night of the attack. I know nothing about the scrolls."

"Isn't she at that hiding place of hers?" Sanfu asked. "The one where she keeps her enormous pet."

"No," Mong replied. "She's disappeared. So has her snake."

AnGangseh has a pet snake? Seh thought. *Interesting.* He considered the snake on his wrist, which was anything but a pet. *Well, if her snake is gone, perhaps she collected it and went to hide somewhere else. That's a good sign.*

Sanfu sat back in his chair. "That's the only news I have to share. I reported everything else to NgGung when he slipped into the village a week ago."

Seh frowned. *That's how Mong knew Sanfu would be traveling with us,* he thought. *I can't believe NgGung snuck in and out of the village without saying hello to us. Sanfu should have given us an update on the bandits, too.* Seh felt his heart begin to beat faster. He was irritated. He took a slow, calming breath.

Sanfu looked at Mong. "Do you have any news to share with me?"

"As a matter of fact, I do," Mong replied. "NgGung is looking into it as we speak, but we have heard news that Ying is in prison and Tonglong now controls his troops—"

The news was so unexpected, Seh's breath caught in his throat. Mong fell silent and stared at the medallion.

Seh knew he'd been caught. Embarrassed, he pivoted

the medallion all the way up and poked his head inside. He nodded hello.

Everyone in the room burst into laughter.

"You must be Mong's son, Seh," the Governor said with a smile. "I am the governor of this region."

"I figured it out," Seh said, lowering his head. "It's nice to meet you."

"The pleasure is mine," the Governor said.

"You're blushing, Seh," Mong said.

Seh raised his head. "Sorry."

Mong chuckled. "Don't be sorry. You did well. You found a hole in our security. The iron latch that secures that medallion must have rusted loose. I'll mention it to Yuen."

Seh shrugged.

"How long have you been up there?" Mong asked.

"Long enough," Seh replied.

"I see," Mong said. "I'm sorry if you're feeling like you've been kept in the dark. We're discussing something that is much bigger than the destruction of Cangzhen or even the destruction of Shaolin. It's a problem that may extend well beyond this region. The new emperor is making life unlivable for everyone except a select few, and we've vowed to do something about it. The Emperor knows about me, but he knows nothing about the Governor's involvement. Nor does he know anything about the Jade Phoenix, Sanfu, or you boys. We'd like to keep it that way."

"I understand," Seh said.

"Good," Mong said. "I'm afraid you can't stay up there any longer. I don't want to risk anyone seeing you. I promise I'll fill you and your brothers in this evening. We could use your help."

Seh's narrow eyes widened. "You could use *our* help?"

"Absolutely," Mong said. "And we'll return the favor. Sanfu has gotten word to me that you wish to address issues surrounding Ying and someone called Bing. I believe I can help you. Ying is in prison, but Bing roams the streets. Bing is indeed the cause of Malao's father's disappearance. I may also be able to find out more about your dragon scroll map through my network. What do you say?"

"Sure," Seh replied.

"Good," Mong said. "We need a few more hours. Perhaps you would like to roam around the water-front until we're through."

Seh thought about the crowds. And the stench. "I don't know—"

"Give it a try," Mong suggested. "Perhaps the bridge—you can see everything from there, and there is usually a breeze over the river, bringing fresh air from outside the city. Do you think you can find it?"

Seh decided to take a look. "I think so," he replied.

"Good," Mong said. "Go eat, then take Fu and Malao there. I'll meet you as soon as we're done. There will be plenty of things to keep you occupied until I arrive, I'm sure. Besides the dragon boats, I recommend you take a look at some of the acrobats. They are extremely talented. There is one group that dresses head to toe in ivory silk that you should find particularly interesting."

"This is amazing!" Malao squealed.

"You can say that again," Fu said.

"This is amazing!" Malao squealed again, and giggled so loud, passersby stared at him.

Seh shook his head. For once, Malao wasn't overreacting. It *was* an amazing sight. From where they stood on the bridge, they could see the activity on both banks of the Yellow River. A hundred dragon boat teams were making preparations to race. About half the boats cruised the water. The rest were beached in neat rows on both the northern and southern shorelines.

The boats were all very long and narrow and rode low in the water. Each had a wooden dragon head attached to the front and a wooden dragon tail attached to the back. Ten men paddled on each side, while a person in the front beat a small drum to keep time so the paddlers would work as one. An additional person in the back steered.

Every boat was different, from the shape of the dragon heads and tails to the colorful patterns on the boats to the costumes worn by the participants. From what Seh could tell from listening to conversations around them on the bridge, the dragon boats came from villages far and near, up and down the river.

Seh knew that dragons were creatures of the water as well as the heavens. He couldn't help but think of Long and wonder if he was okay. Knowing Long, he would be just fine.

Seh inhaled deeply. The warm afternoon breeze washed through his lungs. Mong was right—the bridge was the best spot. They could see the whole riverbank, and it wasn't too crowded. It was large enough to hold several hundred people, but only fifty or so were on it now. It was far less hectic than either shore, where hundreds of people were beginning to stake out positions for the races. They stood shoulder to shoulder under rows of evenly spaced willow trees.

"Hey, what are they doing?" Malao asked. He pointed to a group of people throwing fist-sized packages into the river from the southern shore.

A fat older man standing next to Malao answered. "Those are food offerings."

Fu's ears perked up. "Food?"

The man laughed, and Seh noticed the man's stomach jiggle beneath his brown robe. He was huge. There was a roll of fat beneath his chin the size of a small melon.

"A boy after my own heart," the man said to Fu. "What a waste, eh? Inside those lovely bamboo-leaf packages are special rice-and-meat dumplings."

Fu's eyes widened. "Who are the offerings for?"

"You don't *know*?" the man asked.

"No," Fu replied.

"What do you think this festival is all about?" the man asked.

"Dragon boats," Malao said. "It's the Dragon Boat Festival."

The man shook his sizable head.

Seh decided to join the conversation. He was worried about what Malao and Fu might accidentally say to the stranger. "The boats are only part of it," Seh said to Malao. "This festival is actually called the Duan Wu Festival. Duan Wu was a statesman and poet who lived more than fifteen hundred years ago. In an act of protest against the corrupt rulers of the time, he publicly drowned himself in the river. The dragon boats represent the local fishermen's scramble to try and save the man they loved and respected, and the food and drums recount how the locals beat drums and threw food in the water afterward to keep fish from eating Duan Wu's body."

"Yuck," Malao said.

"I suppose it is a rather morbid story," the large man said. He looked at Seh. "You know your history. Is this your first time here?"

Seh wasn't sure how to answer that. As his mind began to race, a number of drums started beating on the southern shore. They sounded much bigger than the drums on the dragon boats. Fast, rhythmic melodies filled the air, and people both on that shore and the bridge began to move toward the sound. Seh was grateful for the interruption.

"What's going on?" Malao asked.

"Lion dancers," the man replied. "You have heard of lion dancers, haven't you?"

"Of course!" Malao said.

"You should have a look, then," the man said. "The group of acrobats camped over there do the best lion dances I've ever seen. They wear all white."

Seh's eyebrows rose. That's what Mong had said, too. Seh wasn't eager to join the crowd, but his curiosity was piqued.

"I love to dance!" Malao said. "Come on!" He began to wiggle and shake, twisting his way through the people on the bridge.

Fu rolled his eyes and looked at Seh. Seh nodded.

"Nice talking to you boys," the large man said with a grin.

"Likewise," Seh replied.

Fu grunted and began to shove his way through the crowd to keep up with Malao. Seh followed in Fu's wake. As the crowd thickened, Seh paid extra attention to the scroll in the small of his back and the snake on his arm. He didn't want to lose either.

By the time they reached the southern shore, the crowd had formed a huge circle. Malao wriggled and Fu shoved until the three of them were at the circle's inner edge. In the very center, Seh saw two costume creatures that resembled stylized lions he had previously only heard about. A single person was inside one, and two people were inside the other. The lion dancers were hunched over inside the costumes, their legs covered with material that matched the shaggy fringe of the costume lion.

As Seh watched the performers jump, tumble, and gyrate to the beat of the drums, the pit of his stomach began to tingle in a familiar way. He glanced around, and his attention was drawn to a slim girl in an ivory silk dress with a matching turban on her head. She seemed familiar.

Seh eyed the girl as she worked her way around the inner section of the circle with a large bowl in one hand, collecting donations. She moved gracefully and had pale skin and a long, slender neck. She had obviously been injured recently because her other arm was in a sling and she walked with a noticeable limp. Much of her face was covered by an ivory veil, but Seh knew exactly who she was.

"Hok!" Malao shrieked.

Hok turned and hobbled away, ignoring Malao's call.

"Hey!" Malao said. "Why did Hok—*mmmpf!*"

Seh clamped one hand over Malao's mouth and whispered in Malao's ear, "Hok probably doesn't want anyone to know who she is. The bandits told us that people think she is responsible for the destruction of Shaolin Temple. Remember?"

Malao nodded, and Seh let go. Seh watched Hok's white turban slowly bob into the crowd as she limped along. She was leaving the circle.

Fu leaned toward Seh. "What should we do?"

"Follow her," Seh whispered, "and try not to attract any attention."

Fu began to work his way through the masses. Seh

and Malao trailed behind. Hok appeared to know they were following her because she took her time weaving her way through the group. Once she made it out the other side of the circle, she ambled toward a collection of large carts several hundred paces downstream from the crowd. Hok stopped when she reached the makeshift camp's fire pit. She turned to Seh, Malao, and Fu and smiled.

"Can I talk yet?" Malao asked.

Seh nodded.

"Woo-hoo!" Malao said, and jumped into the air. "You're alive, big sister!"

Hok bowed and removed her veil. Her face was badly bruised. "Hello, brothers," she said. She straightened her dress and looked at Seh. "I guess everyone knows my secret now."

"Not everyone," Seh replied. "Only these two. I'm glad you're okay."

Hok stared at Seh, unblinking.

"Seh didn't tell us you were a girl," Fu said. "We found out from that leopard monk Tsung when the three of us were at Shaolin. I'm glad you survived the attack."

Hok's thin eyebrows rose. "You went to Shaolin?"

"Yes," Seh said. "How did *you* end up there?"

"I'll have to tell you some other time," Hok replied. "Right now, I want to introduce you to some people." She cleared her throat and gave a single sharp trill, like a crane.

A moment later, a tall, beautiful woman drifted toward them from within the circle of people upstream.

She was dressed just like Hok, and she looked Seh, Malao, and Fu over with unblinking eyes before stopping beside Hok. "Yes?" she said in a quiet, peaceful voice.

"Mother, I would like you to meet my brothers," Hok said. She pointed. "This is Seh, this is Malao, and this is Fu. Everyone, meet my mother."

Seh blinked. The woman did look a surprising amount like Hok, especially with them both wearing matching head wraps.

Seh bowed.

"Your mother?" Malao said. "Wow! Nice to meet you!"

"Yes," Fu said. "Nice to meet you."

"The pleasure is mine," Hok's mother replied.

"Hey!" a young voice shouted. "What are all those *boys* doing here?"

Seh turned to see the outer edge of the circle part. A girl about five years old ran toward them. Jogging next to her was the single lion dancer from the performance, still in full costume.

The girl ran up to Hok's mother, while the lion dancer stopped next to Hok. The lion dancer put his arm—which looked like a lion's front leg—around Hok's waist. Seh felt his face suddenly flush. What did that dancer think he was doing?

The little girl stomped her foot. "Isn't anybody going to answer my question?"

"Mind your manners," Hok's mother said. She rested her hand on the girl's head, and Seh noticed that the girl's hair was brown. He had never seen anyone with brown hair before. And although the little girl's eyes were Chinese in shape, their color was light brown instead of dark brown or black like everybody else's.

"These boys are your sister's friends," Hok's mother said to the girl.

"You have a sister, too?" Malao said. "That's great!"

Hok nodded, smiling.

Seh pointed at the lion dancer. "Is this your brother?"

"Hardly," the lion dancer replied. At least, that's what Seh thought he said. It was difficult to tell because the dancer spoke with a thick accent Seh didn't recognize. The lion dancer removed the costume head, and Seh did a double take.

It was a teenage boy with very pale skin—even paler than Hok's. He had small red dots and splotches across his nose and cheeks, and his hair was almost white, like rice. Stranger still were his eyes, which were almost completely round, like the moon when it was full. And they were blue. Like the sky. He was so . . . ugly.

"You're a *guai lo*!" Malao said in Cantonese.

The boy didn't respond.

"You're a *ghost boy*," Seh said in Mandarin, and the boy's round eyes narrowed. He took a step toward Seh.

Hok put her hand on the ghost boy's shoulder. "This is Charles," she said.

"What's a 'Charles'?" Fu asked.

"*Charles* is his name," Hok said. "He's my friend, so be nice to him."

Charles stared hard at Fu. Fu growled.

The pit of Seh's stomach began to tingle, and the snake on his arm shivered. Seh focused on Charles, but he didn't sense anything. Something else was wrong. There was a commotion behind them.

The boys turned toward the river, and Seh noticed that five of the dragon boat teams that had been practicing had beached their boats on the southern shore, about two hundred paces from Hok's camp. The team members were coming ashore quickly, and they were lining up in ranks—like soldiers. People in the crowd began to stare and point.

A solitary dragon boat remained in the water behind the men in formation. The steersman stood up and removed his silk hat ceremoniously. A long, thick ponytail braid flopped out and bounced off his chest. He smiled at Seh and shouted across the space between them, "Remember me?"

Seh stared at the man but didn't respond. The man felt extremely familiar.

"Tonglong!" Fu said.

"Very good, Pussycat," Tonglong shouted. "Now it's the serpent's turn to talk. You have something that I want. Give it to me and we'll be on our way. Deny me and—"

Tonglong snapped his fingers. The twenty costumed men in his boat each raised a *qiang* and pointed it at Seh.

CHAPTER
31

The entire southern shoreline erupted into chaos. The crowd dispersed in a thousand directions like an exploding firework. Women and children screamed and men cried out as they slipped and fell and were trampled by hundreds of fleeing feet. Desperate voices of every pitch and volume implored the heavens to protect them from the *qiang*s.

Seh scanned his immediate surroundings. Next to him were Fu, Hok, Hok's mother, Hok's little sister, and Charles. Malao was gone.

Seh began to scan farther out. Most of the people were heading away from the river onto the main thoroughfare, ducking into the side streets that intersected it. At the same time, a group of five individuals was heading in the opposite direction—directly toward him. Seh turned his focus on them. It was Mong, Sanfu, Hung, Gao, and NgGung.

"Don't give up that scroll!" Mong shouted to Seh, his deep, booming voice overpowering the shrieks and cries of the panicked crowd.

Seh's eyes narrowed, and he turned back to face Tonglong. Though they were greatly outnumbered, Seh felt invigorated by the arrival of the bandits. "I didn't plan to," he shouted.

Tonglong tucked his long ponytail braid into his sash. "I had a feeling you would say that," he shouted. He raised one arm high, then let it drop. "FIRE!"

Twenty *qiang*s rang out from Tonglong's dragon boat, and scrambling bystanders howled as *qiang* balls tore into them. Seh blinked several times and glanced around. No one he knew had been hit, though he wasn't sure about Malao. The screaming of the bystanders intensified, and the snake shimmied up Seh's arm. It tightened its grip as the ranks of soldiers surged forward from the riverbank and the men in Tonglong's boat began to reload.

"*Crane Defends the Nest!*" Mong shouted, and before Seh knew it, the bandits had formed a ring around him, Fu, Hok, Hok's sister, and Charles. Seh stared wide-eyed when he noticed Hok's mother had joined the bandits in the ring formation.

"MaMa!" Hok's sister shouted. "No!"

"Shhh," Hok said to her. "MaMa is going to be all right."

Hok's mother didn't respond. Seh watched her stand shoulder to shoulder with the bandits as the first rush of soldiers hit them. Hok's mother fought with the deadly precision and smooth flow of a crane-style master. She delivered an endless barrage of elbow strikes and crane-beak blows to shocked soldiers, leaving them bloodied and broken at her feet. The pile soon grew so large before her that the bandits had to rotate to give her more room.

The other bandits did their fair share, too. Hung swung his mighty war hammers while Sanfu swung his huge tiger-claw fists. Gao barked and kicked, and NgGung taunted his attackers by daring them to punch him in the stomach before following through with vicious spinning back fists. Mong simply waited for an attacker to step within his reach, then squeezed the life out of them.

"Let me fight!" Fu roared.

"NO!" Sanfu said.

Seh turned and saw Fu attempt to rush out of the ring of bandits, between Hung and Sanfu. Fu's eyes were fixed on Sanfu, and it appeared as though Fu never saw Hung's huge, hairy elbow coming. The elbow slammed into the side of Fu's head, and Fu dropped to the ground, out cold. Seh cringed. That was going to leave a mark.

As the bandits fought off wave after wave of attackers, Seh began to worry. The soldiers with the *qiang*s would finish reloading soon. And there was still no sign of Malao. Seh turned to Hok. "I need to know what's going on. *Snake Slithers Up the Tree!*"

Hok bobbed her head once and dropped into a shallow horse stance. Seh stepped onto one of her legs and shimmied up her narrow back until his knees rested on her shoulders. Hok straightened her legs and stood—on her tiptoes.

"Hey!" Charles said. "You're going to hurt her!"

"I doubt it," Seh said. He felt Hok fumbling with something and looked down. Hok's turban had come unraveled. She pulled the entire wrap off her head, and Seh nearly tumbled off her shoulders. Hok's hair was brown! Just like her little sister's!

Seh felt the pit of his stomach begin to tingle, and he looked over at Tonglong's boat. His eyes widened. "Malao!" he shouted. "Look out!"

Shouting proved to be useless. Malao was in the boat with Tonglong and the soldiers, jumping around like crazy, throwing *qiangs* into the water and swinging his monkey stick. Malao's upper lip was curled back. He was out of control. Seh watched helplessly as a brown arm rose up out of the water next to Malao.

Except the arm never came in contact with Malao. Instead, it wrapped around the neck of the man next to Malao and yanked the man over the side.

The eel twins! Seh thought.

But his excitement was short-lived. Malao leaped to the front of the boat, where the drummer usually sat, and froze as he locked eyes with a man sitting in one of the frontmost seats. It was the fat man from the bridge.

Malao's back was to the very front of the boat, and Seh saw a tiny person in a black hood slowly rise up behind Malao from beneath the drummer's seat.

"MALAO!" Seh shouted, and this time Malao

heard him. Malao looked to the shore and was hit in the back of the neck with the fastest snake-head fist Seh had ever seen.

Malao went limp.

And the boat began to move.

Seh's heart leaped into his throat. "My mother!" he shouted. "She's with Tonglong! They have Malao and—"

Tonglong raised one arm and let it fall. "FIRE!"

The *BOOM!* of the *qiang*s was followed by shouts from the bandits.

Hung stumbled backward, gripping his shoulder. Blood seeped between his hairy fingers.

Sanfu roared, clutching his cheek with one hand.

"RETREAT!" Mong shouted.

Hok tilted her head down and dropped her shoulders, sending Seh sliding forward off the slippery white silk of her dress. Seh landed hard on his knees.

Hok grabbed her little sister, and Sanfu scooped up Fu.

"But—" Seh began to say.

"MOVE!" Mong hissed. He grabbed the back of Seh's collar and heaved him forward. Seh stumbled, but someone grabbed his arm and held him steady until he regained his stride. Grateful, Seh looked over and saw that it was Hok's mother.

"Run," she said in an eerily peaceful tone. "You must run."

"I know," Seh said as he picked up his pace. "But they have Malao—"

Hok's mother nodded.

Seh knew Hok's mother was right. There was nothing they could do right now. Seh thought about his own mother and ground his teeth. He adjusted the scroll at his back and felt the snake on his arm tighten its grip.

"Thank you," Seh said to Hok's mother. "I really mean it. My brothers and I have so many enemies, it's difficult to know who to trust. Thank you . . . ah . . . ah . . . I don't even know your name."

As they ran, Hok's mother folded her hands like a Cangzhen monk. She spoke with an icy calm.

"My name is Bing."

Turn the page
for a preview
of the fourth book in
THE FIVE ANCESTORS . . .

CRANE!

CHAPTER
1

Twelve-year-old Hok sat perched high in a tree in a dreamlike state. All around her, Cangzhen was burning. Thick black smoke rushed over her on currents of air formed by the intense heat below. Her brothers, Fu, Malao, Seh, and Long, had already taken flight. It was time for her to do the same. Grandmaster had told them to scatter into the four winds, so into the wind she would go.

Hok spread her arms wide and let the warm, rising air lift her into the night sky. She welcomed the familiar feeling and soon found herself soaring through the darkness, circling higher and higher. Yet no matter how high she flew, she couldn't escape the smoke. It burned her eyes and obscured her vision. She had no choice but to descend once more. Maybe she could somehow fly around the trouble.

Below her, the Cangzhen compound came into view again. Through the smoky haze, Hok saw the outlines of a hundred fallen monks. She was as powerless to help them now as she had been during the attack. She frowned, and continued on.

Hok headed for Cangzhen's main gates and saw her former brother Ying just beyond them, his carved dragon face contorted into an angry scowl. Grandmaster was with Ying, and so was her brother Fu. Hok watched as Ying cut Fu's cheek with his chain whip, then blasted a large hole clear through Grandmaster's upper body with a *qiang*.

Hok shuddered and blinked, and Ying disappeared like mythical dragons were rumored to do. Fu ran away, and Grandmaster slumped to the ground.

Behind her, Hok heard her youngest brother, Malao, giggle. She glanced back, but saw no sign of him. Instead, she caught a glimpse of a monkey demon dancing across a burning rooftop—

What is going on? Hok wondered. She had had strange, vivid dreams before, but never one quite like this. Everything was so clear and so . . . violent.

The images got worse.

Hok saw Grandmaster suddenly stand, streams of smoke drifting in and out of the bloody hole in his chest. He glanced up at Hok soaring overhead, and his wrinkled bald head tumbled off his shoulders.

Hok shuddered again. She had had enough. She wanted to wake up. She pinched herself—and felt it—but nothing changed. She was still gliding on smoky currents of air. She felt as if she were asleep and awake at the same time.

Perhaps the smoke had something to do with it. If she could just get away from the smoke, maybe she could find a way to wake up. Hok glided beyond the tree line, skimming the treetops. She flew as low as possible, hoping that the drifting smoke would rise above her.

She hadn't gotten very far into the forest when she passed over a large hollow tree and caught a glimpse of herself burying Grandmaster's headless body inside it. Curious, Hok landed on a nearby limb and watched herself finish the job, then drift off to sleep inside the tree.

As Hok stared through the smoky darkness, she saw a soldier

with the head of a mantis sneak into the tree hollow and sprinkle something over her sleeping face.

She had been drugged. That was why she was having trouble waking up.

With this realization came a dizzying sensation. Part of Hok's mind raced back to her lessons with Grandmaster concerning certain types of mushroom spores and different plant matter that, if inhaled, could put a person into a dreamlike fog for days on end. Hok grew certain that she was now only half-asleep, which meant that she was half-awake. She made a conscious effort to pull herself into the waking world, and the smoke around her began to thin.

At the same time, Hok watched the soldier's impossible insect head in her dream. It transformed from that of a mantis into that of a man, and she recognized him. His name was Tonglong. He was Ying's number one soldier. Hok watched Tonglong lift her unconscious body and carry it out of the tree hollow.

Hok spread her arms in her dream and leaped into the air, following Tonglong. She glanced down and saw that two soldiers were now carrying her unconscious body along a trail. She was bound and hanging from a pole like a trophy animal.

Hok blinked and the scene below changed. She was now unbound, having a conversation in the forest with Fu, Malao, and a . . . tiger cub?

Hok blinked again, and a stiff breeze rose out of nowhere. It whisked the remaining smoke away, and the images went with it.

When the breeze stopped, Hok felt herself begin to tumble from the sky. She pinched herself again.

This time, she opened her eyes.

Hok found herself facedown on the muddy bank of a narrow stream. The earth was cool and moist, but the midday sun overhead warmed her bare feet and the back of her aching head. She raised her long, bony fingers to the top of her pounding temples and felt something she hadn't felt in years: hair. It was little more than stubble, and caked with mud, but it was undeniable.

How long have I been asleep? Hok wondered. *Where am I?*

She lifted her head and her vision slowly gained focus. So did her other senses.

Hok twitched. She wasn't alone.

"You've been drugged," a voice purred from overhead. "Let me help you."

Hok looked into a nearby tree and her eyes widened. Lounging on a large limb was a lean bald man in an orange monk's robe. The man raised his bushy eyebrows and leaped to the ground with all the grace and nimbleness of a leopard. He approached Hok with smooth, confident strides.

"Dream Dust, I'm guessing," the man said. "If so, you'll be feeling the effects on and off for days. It's powerful stuff. It blurs the line between dreams and reality."

Hok stared, unblinking, at the man. If she remembered her training correctly, Dream Dust was derived from the pods of poppy flowers. Powerful stuff indeed.

"My name is Tsung," the man offered. "It's Mandarin for 'monk.' A simple name for a simple man. I am from Shaolin Temple originally, but I live outside the temple now among regular folk. Hence, my name."

Hok continued to stare.

"You don't say much, do you?" Tsung said. He stopped several paces from her, keeping a respectful distance. "That's just as well. I'll tell you what I know. I spied on your captors, Major Ying and Tonglong, for quite some time. I make a habit of keeping an eye on things in this region. I had a feeling you were something special, even before I realized you were from Cangzhen. And once

I overheard them discussing the fact that you were a girl, well, let's just say that I was doubly impressed. For fighters as skilled as Ying and Tonglong to go to such lengths to bind and drug such a young captive, that's extraordinary."

Hok glanced at her wrists and ankles. They were raw and coated with dried blood, but she didn't feel a thing. The Dream Dust must be numbing the pain.

Tsung nodded at her. "Interesting outfit you're wearing. It appears large enough to fit a grown man."

Hok looked at her oversized robe and ill-fitting orange pants. She'd always worn clothes that were too large in preparation for the days when loose clothes would better hide her gender. It seemed that didn't matter anymore. She shrugged. She didn't know what to say.

"You really aren't doing so well, are you?" Tsung asked.

Hok shook her head. The movement made her dizzy, and her vision began to tunnel.

"I'm taking you to Shaolin," Tsung said. "I have a horse near-by, and we will be there in no time. I'll take care of you." He flashed a toothy grin, and Hok sensed something beneath the surface. Something sinister. He took a step toward her.

Hok formed a crane-beak fist with her right hand, bunching the tips of all four fingers together and pressing them tightly against the tip of her thumb.

Tsung's smile faded. "A crane stylist?" he said. "I should have guessed."

Hok didn't offer a response.

"They say Dream Dust allows the user to see into the hearts of others," Tsung said. "Do you think this is true?"

Hok didn't respond. The world around her was growing hazy, as if smoke was drifting over her eyes. She felt her crane-beak fist loosen, her fingers relaxing into a limp open hand.

"Very interesting," Tsung purred, his feline grin returning. "Since it appears as though you're about to drift away again, I'll let you in on a little secret. My brothers at Shaolin no longer trust me, either. In fact, they haven't let me into the compound in years. However, that is all about to change. You shall be my ticket in. The ticket for me, and a few thousand of my closest friends."